Empower

Publishing

Also by
from Tamelia Keaton

A Scared Life to a Loving Wife

Rips, Tips and Scripts

from *Empower Publishing*

Struggles
of a Good Wife

By

Tamelia Keaton

Empower Publishing
Winston-Salem

Empower

Publishing

Empower Publishing
302 Ricks Drive
Winston-Salem, NC 27103

First Empower Publishing Books edition published August, 2025
Empower Publishing, Feather Pen, and all production design are trademarks.

For information regarding bulk purchases of this book, digital purchase and special discounts, please contact the publisher at publish.empower.now@gmail.com

Cover design by Miguel Keaton

Manufactured in the United States of America
ISBN 978-1-63066-617-0

Dedications

I want to dedicate this book to women who are wives or waiting to be wives. I want women to know that marriage vows should be taken seriously and no matter what happens in your relationship, God should be at the top of any decision you make. No matter what happens in your marriage, or your relationship, always honor the Lord and his word.

—Tamelia Keaton

1.
LAYLA AND MIKE'S FIRST STRUGGLE

ONE YEAR LATER

Layla woke up to a screaming baby yelling to the top of its lungs. She looked at the clock. It was 3:15 in the morning. Layla jumped out of the bed half-crazy from the dream she was having when she had just fallen asleep an hour ago. Mike was in bed sleeping like he had no care in the world and that he was in a different world and there was no baby around.

Layla went to the room and picked the baby girl up in her arms to comfort her. The pretty little girl was gorgeous. She had curly brown hair already on her shoulders. The baby's eyes were hazel brown like her mother's and when she looked at you, she would have you melting in her glaze. Her skin was silky smooth and a light brown complexion which was a mixture of both her mom and her dad.

Layla wiped the tears from her eyes while comforting her and showing her love. This was night seven of the nightmares and Layla was so tired of not being able to sleep a full night. She was going to mention to Mike that maybe they should take her to the doctor to ensure that she was not having any problems that could be dealt with. Michaela was almost back to sleep, so Layla decided to just stay in her room and fall

1

asleep with her just in case she decided to wake up again.

Layla was awakened by the sun shining in her face. She looked at the clock and it was 7:15 AM in the morning. She jumped up because she of course didn't hear her alarm clock in the other room, and now it was time to help Mike get ready for work. She went into the room and Mike was already in the shower. She spoke to him and asked if he would like some breakfast before he left.

Layla went downstairs to see if the maid had already cooked something. She realized she hadn't, so she asked her to make some oatmeal for the baby and Mike a breakfast sandwich to take with him. Layla had a headache and remembered that she had been so busy taking care of everyone that she didn't eat anything last night and now she had a major headache. She went to the cabinet to get some medicine but was interrupted by Mike calling her saying that Michaela was awake.

Layla again stopped what she was doing to go tend to her daughter. Michaela was in her father's arms getting all his attention. They were so cute together. She was a mix of both of them, but she looked more like her daddy. She's definitely was a daddy's girl and she couldn't do anything wrong in his eyes. He was comforting her but when she saw her mother she reached up her arms to be picked up by her mother.

Layla grabbed her and took her to her room to put some clothes on because she was going to her grandma's house so that Layla could get some things taken care of around the mansion. Layla thought about all the things that she needed to do but probably wouldn't have enough time to do all of them. After she put her baby's clothes on, she took her downstairs to give her breakfast. Mike was coming down the steps at the same time heading towards the kitchen as well. He grabbed and kissed his wife and told her that she looked very tired.

When they all got to the kitchen table Layla was telling Mike how their daughter was not sleeping well and keeps waking up in the middle of the night multiple times. Mike seemed interested, but then his phone started ringing and he was more interested in the work and who was on the phone, at the moment. Layla got upset and decided that she would make their daughter a doctor's appointment today so that she can at least try to get some rest. Her headache wasn't getting any better, so Layla ate a little and took some medicine to ease the pain. Layla wanted Mike to make some time so that they could talk about him helping out a little more with their daughter, especially so that she could get some rest at night so she didn't look so tired.

Lately it seemed that Mike just wanted her to stay at home and be a housewife and not pursue her dreams or even go back to school to get her master's degree. After the incident about 2 years ago he seemed to want to be a little overprotective of her, which was making Layla feel a little trapped. The only thing Layla had been doing lately was being a wife to his needs, a mother to Michaela and going to church to be around her sisters at church. Layla's sisters were both in relationships and in their ideal careers and Layla's best friends were planning weddings and working in their ideal careers. Since Layla had the baby, she seemed to be the only one that had given up on her dreams which were causing a little stress in her life. She had started to have more panic attacks and had an appointment set up to go see a therapist so that she could learn how to get a balance in her life.

Layla thanked God every day that the Lord had blessed her with a wonderful husband who was also a great provider and a good father to his daughter, however things had changed in their relationship which included them not being able to spend much time because of their baby and his work schedule. Most of the time together was when her husband wanted to be intimate which Layla didn't feel like doing that in the first place. It wasn't that it was bad or something, but it was more on the times he wanted to do it. After she got done with getting everyone else happy Layla was tired and didn't feel like making love to her husband. She just wanted to relax and do absolutely nothing.

Layla didn't know that marriage life and motherhood were so hard. She realized that her life had moved very fast because they wanted to honor God and wait until they were married but Layla realized that she was not ready to be a mother. She wanted to do things that she wanted to do and that didn't include having to care for a little one. She loved her daughter but didn't know what she was going to have to do to be able to get a balance with her life and being a good wife. Layla took a mental note to write this down so that she could see if her therapist could give her any advice.

It seemed like everyone around her was busy in their own world and that Layla was in a totally different world. Was this what depression felt like? Layla had lots of questions but not enough answers, so she decided to deal with it later.

Layla was deep in thought when she heard Mike calling her name and letting her know that he would drop Michaela off at daycare on his way to work and she said that would be great. She kissed her husband and her daughter and told them that she would see them later. Layla was looking forward to a day by herself and maybe she could get a nap and catch up on some much-needed rest. She might even call to see if Felicia could do her hair. She hadn't been in a month due to the lack of sleep. This would be a great opportunity to pamper herself and not have to worry if her family was okay or not.

2.
TIME FLIES WHEN YOU'RE HAVING FUN

Layla didn't realize that she had so many things to do. She had to go grocery shopping, do laundry, pay the bills and ensure that the accountant had budgeted things right. She also was able to accomplish getting her hair done, getting a pedicure and getting a little quick nap. It was already 2:00 in the afternoon and she noticed that time was flying because there were only three hours left before she had to get the baby from daycare. She decided that she could lay down for another hour and that she would set the alarm clock so she wouldn't oversleep to go pick her daughter up from daycare. She went to her room and laid across the bed for some more rest.

She had just got into a good sleep when she heard the doorbell ring downstairs. She waited to see what the maid was going to do and that is when she heard her coming up the stairs saying that it was a guy here saying that Mike had sent him there to do some installations in the panic room. Layla said that it was fine but to have one of the security guards stay with him just in case he had any questions.

She drifted back off to sleep and again was awakened by the alarm clock this time, letting her know that it was time to get up and pick her daughter up. She got up out of the bed and went to the bathroom to get herself together. She put on a pretty dress and some cute flats and grabbed her purse on the way out. Before leaving she decided to see if the gentleman was still doing the installations in the panic room, so she walked downstairs to the basement. She could hear drills and people talking in the room, so she figured that he had a team of workers helping him out.

She opened the door and there she saw a very attractive man maybe in his late 30s managing a team of workers. She hadn't seen a man this handsome since she met Mike. In her mind, she thought that she knew that his wife was lucky to have him just like she was lucky to have Mike. The man immediately noticed her beauty and had the team stop working while he took his opportunity to get a closer look so that he could introduce himself. He said that his name was Mateo, and he was the owner of the Mateo Construction Club. He was very polite and let Layla know that the job would take longer than a day and that they would be back all this week to finish the project.

Layla noticed that he was gazing into her hazel eyes, so Layla started to feel a little uncomfortable. She told him that it was fine and that whatever her husband said was fine with her. Mateo seemed a little disappointed to know that she was the Mrs. of the house and was fast to tell her that her husband was a very lucky man. Layla didn't notice a ring on his finger, so she assumed that he didn't have a wife at home. She let him know that she was on her way out to get her little girl and that she would see him around.

Mateo watched her walk out, mesmerized by her physique and how beautiful she was. He could tell that she was an athlete because she was definitely in shape and was carrying all her weight in the right places. Mateo wasn't usually moved by women, but this woman had all his attention, and he wasn't ready to give up hope yet. Mateo knew he was a nice-looking man and that every woman threw themselves at him married or single. He didn't see her any differently. He knew that he would have to be careful because she had a husband, but if he played his cards right, she would give him everything he wanted and more even if she was married.

Layla hopped in the car and got on the highway to try to beat the 5:00 traffic rush on the highway. Of course, everyone was getting off of work and trying to get home and everyone was driving like bats out of the cage trying to get to where they wanted to go.

Layla arrived at the school and parked her car. She went in to sign her daughter out of the classroom. This was a private daycare, and they didn't play any games about breaking any rules. They were strict when it came to following all the laws. They understood that the children who attended there were privileged and that was the reason they were in business and making good money. Mike ensured that his daughter got the best care because he really didn't want her to go to school at all. He wanted Layla to watch their daughter full-time, but Layla convinced him that she should be around other children, and that she needed a break to be able to do things around the house so she wouldn't be overwhelmed. Mike finally agreed but made sure the daycare was the best in the world.

Michaela's teacher said that she seemed very tired today and didn't want to really participate in the activities much. Layla told them that she had been waking up multiple times during the night and that she was going to call the doctor to get her an appointment. Laya thanked the teacher for letting her know and said that she would see her tomorrow.

They walked to the car, and she put Michaela in her car seat and asked her if she would like to get some ice cream. Michaela was very happy to hear the word ice cream, so they went to the parlor and sat down and ate a little ice cream together.

They were both beautiful and everyone would always give her compliments on how pretty the little girl was and that she looked like her mother. Layla was used to getting stares from both men and women because a lot of people knew who she was married to but also because she was just that pretty.

They both finished their ice cream and Layla wanted to get back home so that she could start cooking dinner for that night. She knew she could just get the maid to do it but occasionally, she liked to cook for her husband. She planned on making him a steak, homemade loaded baked potatoes and broccoli. She would also make some bread and brownies because she knew that her husband loved sweets.

Layla finally got through all the traffic on the highway. She got back to the driveway and hit the button to open the gate and went to her parking space.

She noticed that Mike wasn't home yet, which wasn't unusual because it wasn't even 6 yet. Mike normally would get home around 6:30 in the evening because he and his friends would go get a 30-minute workout after work at the gym. Mike was always keeping his physique intact and that was one thing that Layla loved about her husband.

When she hit the garage, she could still hear the men doing work in the panic room. Layla was getting out of the car and getting the baby out of the car seat when she heard Mateo asking her if she needed any help. Layla said no and that she was fine and that's when Mateo saw the prettiest little girl he had ever seen. He spoke to the girl and asked Layla what her name was. Layla told him the baby's name and she guided the girl into the house to her playroom by the kitchen. This was a room that she created that was kid proof and she had toys and everything she needed to play with in a safe environment. The maid noticed they were back, and she immediately came to relieve Layla of the baby.

Layla asked if they were finishing up for today, but Mateo was too busy staring at her beauty. Layla got an uncomfortable feeling and decided to cut the conversation short to start cooking. She told Mateo that she had to get going because time was going by too fast. Mateo agreed and said that he and the crew were going to get to a good stopping point and pick up tomorrow at 10 in the morning.

Layla said that she would see him tomorrow, but Mateo watched as Layla walked into the kitchen to start dinner. Layla didn't know anything about him, and she made a note to make sure that her husband checked his background to ensure he was legit, and that Michaela and she would be safe around him.

Time was flying by, so she had to finish dinner before her husband came home because she knew that he would be very hungry. She felt that she could probably eat well tonight too and not go to sleep hungry again like she did last night. That headache was no joke which was a result of when she had the baby, and she was leaking spinal fluid from her brain because of the little hole in her spine. The headache was excruciating which caused her to have to stay another night in the hospital so that they could do a blood patch and cover up the hole. The doctors told her that Coca Cola helped with spinal headaches which was why she loved drinking soda any chance she got.

Layla was putting the finishing touches on dinner when she heard the garage going up and her husband coming into the side door. He called for her and she told him that she was in the kitchen. She had already put the baby in the highchair and had her food cut up and cooled so that she could feed herself. Layla told her husband to go wash his hands for dinner and she would fix their plates and put them on the table.

Mike came down and kissed her and sat down at his spot ready to say the blessings so that they could eat the wonderful meal she prepared. Mike told her that he loved it when she cooked for him, and he knew that it was going to be good. The meal didn't disappoint, and they were talking to one another about their day.

They started to talk about Michaela, and the daycare and that she had already had their little girl an appointment to see the doctor. Mike agreed that it would be good and then he asked about the contractors.

Layla told him about Mateo and asked questions of whether he did a background check to ensure their safety. He told him that Mateo was the one who designed the mansion and did the panic room and that they were first cousins on his mother's side. Layla now knew why something was familiar about him and why he was so handsome. She mentioned that he was kind of giving her vibes as if he liked her and Mike assured her that she had nothing that she had to worry about. Layla left it like that and figured that her husband knew best.

Time was really flying, and it was already after 8 PM. It was bathtime for the baby and Layla had every intention of getting her to bed early tonight and maybe getting some quality time with her husband. After she got the baby settled in bed Layla walked into the room and heard the shower running in their bathroom. Layla shut the door and took her clothes off to get into the shower with her husband.

3.
GO AWAY BAD DREAMS

Layla was awakened again by her daughter calling her name and whining. She woke up and noticed that the sun was not even shining yet outside, meaning that everyone was still sleeping. Layla let out a sigh of frustration and made a mental note that she was going to make her baby an urgent appointment because these nights were getting longer and longer, and she still hadn't slept right in the last three months.

Layla walked to her daughter's room, and she was sitting on the side of her bed waiting for her mother to pick her up. She hugged and comforted the little girl and said a prayer for her daughter and their entire household. She started to sing to the little girl a gospel song to soothe her but she was really giving herself some encouragement of going on with her own life. Layla felt her body was on the edge of break and she feared that she didn't know what that meant. She had talked to her husband last year about getting some counseling together and his response was not the one she was hoping for. She loved her man, but she didn't understand why their pride was so on the top that he felt that they both had it all together. For a person looking from the outside, they did have it all together, however there was always room for improvement on the inside. On the inside, Layla felt alone, overworked and not as close to her heavenly Father as she wanted to be. She was going to church every Sunday and Bible study on Tuesdays, but something felt like it was still missing.

Layla was so much in her own thoughts that she didn't realize that her daughter had already fallen back to sleep, so she laid her back down in her bed and tiptoed to her own bed so that she could catch a couple of more hours of sleep because it was only 2:30 in the morning.

Layla got back to bed, only to notice that her husband was in the bathroom talking with someone on the phone. Who was he talking to at this time of the morning and that she hoped it wasn't an emergency with a family member? She went to the bathroom and opened the door only to find him finishing the end of the conversation and hanging up the phone. Layla asked Mike was everything ok? Mike responded that it was his assistant from work discussing some important business matters that needed to be dealt with in the morning.

Layla thought that it was strange, and she knew that Mike wouldn't lie to her, so she ignored it and went back in the room. Mike got back in bed, held her and they both drifted back to sleep. Layla was in a deep sleep when she was welcomed to a dream where she saw Mike talking close to a pretty woman at his office. In the dream she was bringing him lunch and was walking to his office when she saw a pretty, middle-aged woman being very flirtatious with Mike and Mike seemed to be enjoying it. The flirty gestures turned into some intimate touching and in the dream, she interrupted them so that it wouldn't go any further. She was confronting Mike when the woman tried to comment and that is when the old Layla came out and she gave the girl a blow across her face. The lunch went everywhere, and Layla and the woman were having it out. Mike was trying to break it up, but Layla wasn't done giving her the hands. Mike finally pulled Layla off her and that is when the woman told Layla that Mike didn't love her, and that they were in a relationship.

Before Layla could respond in the dream, she was awakened by Mike calling her name asking if she was ok. Layla woke up sweating and even swinging at Mike. Mike grabbed her and took her in his arms. Layla was talking to Mike about the dream and was asking him if she had anything to worry about. Mike assured her that she was all he needed and that they were stuck together for life.

Layla believed him but thought God might be giving her a warning to stay alert. On the other hand, maybe she was just having that dream because she heard him talking to a woman on the phone at not appropriate times of the night. Layla's mother didn't raise any fools so she would watch and pray because she was sure that God was giving her a warning. Layla would also go take Mike some lunch which would also give her a chance to see if anyone was new that looked like the woman in her dream or even if they carried that Jezebel spirit that would love to get that kind of power over her husband. Who wouldn't want her husband who was a man of God, rich, handsome and a good father.

She realized that being a good helpmate or a wife meant looking out for other women who are trying to get too close to her man and she was not going to let that happen. Sometimes men didn't see things like that, especially her husband, because he always wanted to help everyone around him even if it meant getting bit by the snake he was trying to help.

4.
BUSY BUSY BEE

Layla had a lot she needed to get done today including having lunch with her husband. Layla noticed when she walked out of the room, she could hear her husband and daughter already in the kitchen, so she called her husband's secretary and had her to block off his lunch time for her and that she was bringing him lunch. His secretary, Emily, was always so nice and kept her husband on top of his job.

She went downstairs to the kitchen and noticed that the maid had already prepared a full course breakfast. She had a nice spread of waffles, eggs and bacon with fruit on the side and orange juice. The maid, Mary, knew what her daughter's favorites were and these were some of them. She kissed her husband and daughter, and her daughter fed her a piece of her own bacon. Layla ate it and said thanks for feeding her mother.

Mike said that he was going to have to get to work for a big meeting and if she would drop their daughter to daycare. Mike also mentioned that John and the security team were on high alert because two women were reported missing, and they believe that the suspect was still on the run. They thought it would be best if a car followed just to be on the safe side.

Layla didn't argue with her husband because he

knew what was best for her, especially after her scary event that happened two years ago. That was the most terrifying event that had ever happened to her and even though God had delivered her from that fear she was going to assure that she operated in common sense.

Layla was about to start the day when the doorbell rang. Layla went to open the door, and Mateo was standing there staring at her. He spoke to her with his eyes first then his mouth and Layla gave him a dry hello. She let him know that the security guards would be there, and he could start working as soon as he wanted. Layla grabbed her daughter and headed upstairs so that she could put on the finishing touches of her outfit so that she could start her day. She noticed eyes on her when she walked away and decided that she was not going to give him the benefit of the doubt that she had noticed him watching her. It was something about him that creeped her out but after the response that she got from her husband about his cousin she had decided to leave that situation alone.

While Layla was upstairs, she decided to give the child psychologist a call about her daughter and was happy to see that they had an opening later that day.Layla said that she would take the appointment but still decided to take her daughter to school so that she could get the rest of her day completed.

Layla grabbed Michaela and let John from the security team know that she was leaving so he could get a car to trail her. She went to get gas first and then dropped her daughter off at school. After leaving there she stopped by the massage parlor and was able to get a full body massage, manicure and pedicure. Getting that done allowed her to take a short nap as well because her body was feeling very relaxed.

She decided that she could stop by Sam's grocery store and get her cleaning supplies and other snacks that were needed for the house. She was able to pick up all she needed and spent almost $500. The nice employee thought that he could score some brownie points, so he walked out with her to help her load the groceries in the trunk. This alerted the security guard who got out of his car to take over the job so that he could make sure that she was safe. Once this was completed, it was time to pick up lunch for her husband and go to his job. Laya was busy all day but things were flowing with the right times so she would call it a productive day.

While she was waiting for the food to be put in the car she decided to make a call to her advisor at Wake Forest University so that she could start enrolling back into school for her master's program. She was going to get her PhD in psychology no matter what she had to do. Her advisor let her know that all her paperwork and financial aid was complete and that he had already sent her an email about the classes that she should take. Layla was happy to hear that all her things were in place and that she would be starting online classes very soon.

The food finally came out, so she headed to their company to have lunch with her husband. When she got to the job she parked at her spot beside her husband and walked inside the building. The security guard parked but waited in the car knowing that she would be safe in the secured building. Layla got to her husband's floor and was walking toward his office when something felt very familiar.

She was about to open the door when she saw a new face which belonged to a woman hanging too close to her husband at his computer. The middle-aged woman was very attractive which brought the dream back to reality. The warning seemed to be right on time because Layla saw that the lady was very into her husband more than a work relationship.

Layla didn't knock; she walked in and spoke to her husband. The lady seemed surprised; however, her husband immediately came to his wife and did the proper introductions. The lady didn't seem that happy to know that he had a wife, but Layla put her hand out to be polite, offering the mystery woman a handshake. The lady declined the handshake and just spoke to her cordially.

Her husband said that her name was Jameelah, and she was one of the new administrators. Layla made a mental note to keep an eye on her and knew that she would ask her husband if she was the mystery woman in the middle of the night. Jameelah let them know that she had lots of work to do and would talk with him later. Layla watched her walk out with the lady's body language speaking of a Jezebel spirit who was upset that she was interrupted on executing her plan to get what she wanted.

They were having lunch when the question came up whether she was the one calling in the middle of the night. He mentioned that it was her, however, the meeting that was held this morning involved the board and her to let her know that she was out of line and it better not happen again. She received a write up for it and said that she seemed to be on her job better after the meeting was over.

Layla decided just to let her husband know that she needed to be watched, and she also told him about the dream she had the night before. He assured her that she had nothing to worry about, however Layla let her husband know that she trusted him but didn't trust her and that she was only trying to cover him. She also let her husband know that there should always be another person present with her because she has hidden agendas and she didn't want him to have a situation at his job.

He took her advice and then the conversation shifted to their daughter. She let him know that they were able to get their daughter in to be seen today and when she left him, she was going to pick her up early and take her to the therapist. Her husband let her know that he would have to sit this one out but to fill him in with all the details later. He also let her know that he would be home late tonight and to order Chinese for dinner tonight instead of cooking. They said their goodbyes and Layla said that she would see him later after work. Layla realized that she had been busy as a bee but the last thing on the day's list would be the doctor's appointment for her daughter and now ordering Chinese for dinner.

She got to her daughter's school about 20

minutes later to sign her out of school early for the appointment. The teacher seemed really pleased about her daughter seeing a therapist and she asked if she could fill her in later on how it went. Michaela slept all the way there, which was about 20 minutes. Layla proceeded to the back of the car to get her and had to carry her inside for the appointment. Her daughter woke up and was wondering if it was time to get ice cream. She told her if she was good at the appointment they would stop by on the way home to get some. Her daughter said that she promised to do good.

After checking in for the appointment, the psychologist called them from the lobby. They did their introductions and Layla told them why she was there. The more she found out about her daughter, the more Layla knew she needed therapy also. The therapist was so easy to talk to and that Layla decided that she would start seeing her as well. Layla was very relieved when the therapist said that her daughter was perfectly normal but sometimes this happens when the child was so used to getting everything she wanted and the older she gets the better the sleeping will get. She let Layla know what signs to look for if it was getting worse, but she said with Layla being a first-time mom she did good with checking it out anyway. Layla let her know that she would make an appointment for herself also, because she liked her spirit and she seemed easy to talk to.

They said goodbye to each other, and Layla realized it was already after 4 and that she promised the baby ice cream. They arrived at their ice cream parlor and sat in their regular spot sharing sherbert ice cream which was one of her daughter's favorite kinds. She cleaned her daughter up and decided maybe they could still make it home before the highway was a nightmare.

Layla and Michaela walked through the door and the maid grabbed the baby to take her to the playroom for a little while. She noticed that Mateo and his team were still doing work in the panic room. She decided to go and call the food in when her security guard was heading her way saying that the contractors needed to see her. Layla was wondering what they wanted and how much longer they had to go so she headed towards the panic room.

Mateo was anticipating her entering the room and already had sent his boys on a break so he could have some time alone with her. He had to test his theory to see what he was working with. Layla walked through the door and Mateo's eyes were all over her again. Layla immediately became uncomfortable and asked where the rest of his team was. He mentioned that he sent them on a break. She thought it was odd that they went to break at this time of the day and he didn't go with them.

Layla confirmed her fears when he tried to grab her hand and pull her towards his body. Layla pulled back and gave him a disgusted look. She told him that she was not happy with these gestures and that he should have had enough respect for his cousin to not try to hit on her. She also told him that, if he couldn't keep this on a professional level, then she didn't need him around her home anymore. He apologized and said that it wouldn't happen again, and that she was so beautiful he didn't know what came over him.

She left him there and went to continue to get the Chinese food called in for her family. She thought she should tell Mike about it but thought about how he reacted last time and decided to let it go and tell him if it happened again. Layla knew that the weapon would form but it would not prosper and that it was nothing the enemy could do to try to ruin their marriage, not his cousin or his coworker.

Layla was waiting for the dinner to arrive and decided to go play with her daughter in the playroom. Her little girl was busy as a bee. She had her favorite toys everywhere and had Maria all over the place playing with her. Layla figured Maria needed a break, so she went in for the rescue.

Layla and her daughter were having so much fun that she didn't even see that Mateo had found his way watching them in the playroom. Mateo watched as he enjoyed what he was seeing. He loved to see how active she was with her daughter and how beautiful they both were to him. The more he watched the more envious he became. He started to wonder why he hadn't met her first and this would be his life right now. He wondered why his cousin always got better things even when they were growing up? Mateo's mother was far from a saint, and she knew how to use what she had to get what she wanted. Mateo was also an only child on his mom's side, and Mike was like a brother to him. Even though he was five years older than Mike they still had a lot in common.

Mateo would get to stay a lot with Mike because his mother stayed in the streets. He didn't even know his father himself but was told by his mother, who was Mike's mother's sister, that he was dead and was a womanizer who wanted nothing to do with him when he was born. His mother said that his father would run around with a lot of different women, and she wanted nothing to do with him, especially because he was the main reason she ended up on the streets to support herself. His aunt took him in at a young age and raised him like her own son. His Aunt June was always so nice to him and would treat him and her own son the same. When he got older, she made sure he was living right by allowing him to go to whatever college he wanted and giving him everything he needed to start a lucrative construction company. To make matters better, she turned him on to all her rich friends which kept much business to where he needed an entire team to make his business work. Now, he had all he wanted including a mansion on the good side of town, a mansion in New York and a billion-dollar company.

He knew that Layla was probably used to the finer things, but he had no doubt that he could support her better than his cousin could. He had noticed that she was always alone and that she seemed to be raising the girl on her own. Mateo felt he needed another way in because she had made it very clear to him that she didn't want him, however he wasn't done with seeing her yet. Maybe he needed to get busy with talking with his cousin to see how he could get a little closer to her by surprise. He knew how Mike felt about him, and he knew that their family believed to never allow anyone to come between them, so he felt he had the advantage over her. He would give his cousin a call so that he could stay for dinner one night after work. He left to let his crew know that they were done for today and would start back in the morning around 10.

Layla was so busy as a bee with her daughter that she noticed that time was running faster than she could catch it. She remembered that her husband said that he wouldn't be home on time. She heard the door opening and noticed that Maria was coming in with the Chinese food for dinner. She decided to get an early start by getting bathtime out the way before dinner. She decided that it would be faster if she hops in with her daughter to kill two birds with one stone.

She went to get her daughter's bath clothes out of her room and brought her to her jacuzzi bathtub. Michaela loved to act like she was swimming in the bathtub so it would give her some fun while she was taking care of her own bath. Her thoughts drifted about the conversation she had with Mateo but there was something familiar about him, but she didn't know what it was. They finished their baths and put on their clothes to go downstairs to eat dinner.

The whole family loved Chinese, and it saved a lot of time as well. She fixed their plates and was about to eat when she heard her husband coming into the door talking with Mateo. She was boiling inside and realized that he must think of this was like a game so she would bring up the conversation again with her husband.

Mike came over to kiss his wife and then his daughter and asked if she would also fix Mateo a plate. He proceeded to say that he had run into his cousin at the store and invited him back so that they could talk about how the project was going and for him to get to know his wife a little bit better.

Layla was steaming inside because she realized that he was enjoying playing dirty games that included her. This wouldn't be a good time to tell her husband; however, she would bring up the fact that she thought that maybe they should hire someone else to finish the job. Layla felt so uncomfortable at the table. She wanted to be all she could be for her husband but was on the fence not to let Mateo see that. She knew he was only there because of her. It didn't make matters any better that she had just got out of the bathtub and only had on a Victoria's Secret short set, which was not provocative, but it was not enough for her around him. If she knew he was coming, she would have dressed like it was 40 degrees in the house and she was 90 years old.

She kept the conversations short when it was her time to talk, and she paid more attention to her daughter instead of the men. She let them talk as men and had to endure the looks, secretive stares and the sick imagination that was gleaming all over his face while he was playing his game with her.

After about 30 minutes of it all Layla started to not feel good and told her husband to carry on, however she was going to go upstairs and put their daughter in bed and get an early start on some rest.

When she said that Mateo's whole demeanor changed and now, all of a sudden, he had somewhere he needed to be. Layla thought how her husband could not see what was going on and why he was acting so naive. As she headed up the steps she turned back and gave her husband a kiss on his lips and watched Mateo dream that one day it could be him. To make matters worse, Mateo was getting aroused seeing her in the short set. She gave Mateo an evil look before leaving.

She took her daughter and went upstairs and decided to play it safe and put on a house coat. When she got upstairs her breathing was heavy and she needed to calm down because she was feeling an anxiety attack coming alone. What was happening? She hadn't had an attack since she went through her traumatic event about two years ago. She made sure that she would spend time with God so that he could reveal whatever he was trying to get her to see with this situation.

Layla prayed to God and for her family and immediately her breathing got back on track. Layla took her daughter in her room and stayed with her and put on her favorite cartoons.

5.
BE HONEST TO ME

Layla and Michaela were lying in the bed together watching the last of the cartoons when Layla heard the door closing and the alarm being set. She assumed that her husband was letting his perverted cousin out, which she hoped that she wouldn't have to see again. Layla picked Michaela up to take her to her own room so maybe she would have a little talking time with her husband before going to bed.

When she came back, Mike was getting undressed and getting ready for bed. She was about to start a conversation with him when his phone rang, and a female was talking on the phone about something that went on at the end of Mike's workday. Layla let out a sigh of frustration because lately she wanted to get a little attention from her own husband, but lately it seems that she had to share him with the entire world. Layla realized that it was not easy being a wife and that it was a daily process to stay strong to each of the vows, but she was determined to honor her vows with the Lord and her husband no matter what.

Mike seemed to be a little agitated on the phone with whatever was being said. Hopefully she could be a help to whatever would make him ok. He seemed to be coming to the end of his conversation, so Layla continued to wait patiently for her time to speak to him.

When he got off of the phone, he immediately started telling her that it was the Jameelah girl again complaining that something didn't look right in the budgets and that she would need him to look at them with her to ensure the debits and credits were lined up correctly. Mike seemed to not be as interested, and so Layla suggested that he delegate this task to the senior administrator and that he shouldn't be a part of it alone, because Jameelah was wanting more of his personal time. Mike seemed to look at Layla like what she said didn't matter and he said that he would help her with the report.

Layla left it alone because he had just upset her because he wasn't looking at the bigger picture. Layla opted to change the subject and asked him where was he when he ran into Mateo to invite him to dinner. Mike said that he stopped at the store by the house to fill up his gas and Mateo was also there. Layla thought that it was very convenient because he had not too long had a run in with her at their house.

Layla knew that there was something not right, but she couldn't figure it out right now, but she was going to get to the bottom of it. Layla thought that she would try to be honest with her husband so she told him that Mateo tried to make a move on her today, however she let him know that if he couldn't keep it strictly business then they should hire someone to finish the job. She inquired on how much longer did he have to finish the job and that she wasn't comfortable around him. When he wasn't there with her, she mentioned that it was ironic that he ended up at their dinner table not too long after they had the disagreement, when he reached out and tried to grab her and bring her to his arms.

Mike looked at Layla again like she was speaking another language which frustrated her even more. Layla asked Mike to be honest and asked him how much did he really know about his cousin's dad? Mike then went on the defense mode. He defended his cousin by talking about how his life wasn't good because he had to grow up without a father and a mother who was in the streets a lot. He went on to say that Mateo was a good person, who had beaten the odds of being successful despite his situation and that he would never disrespect him like that because they were more like brothers.

Mike had completely overlooked what she had just told him again. This made Layla furious and sad at the same time. Here she was doing all she can to honor the Lord and her husband and now her own husband wouldn't even consider that his cousin was a pervert who was trying to come in the middle of their relationship. Layla let her husband know that she was disappointed with him and if anything happened, he could not say that she didn't try to tell him.

Mike sensed that Layla was getting upset and that her breathing was getting much faster. He immediately tried to calm her down by apologizing to her and saying that he would watch more carefully but his cousin was a good person. Layla realized that he was going to always look out for his family, so she made a point to talk with John in secret to do her own background check on him. She knew that he had the same last name as her mother-in-law before she had married, so she figured that it was a start. She got on her knees and prayed and let her husband know that she had forgiven him and that she didn't want to go to bed mad at him.

Mike must have thought that meant that they could cuddle with each other, but Layla didn't have that in mind at all. She told him goodnight and that she would see him in the morning because she was tired and had a lot on her mind. She forgave him but she hadn't forgotten that he took his cousin's side over hers which made her out of the mood to cuddle with him anyway.

Honestly, Layla was feeling that she and Mike were growing apart slowly and that counseling with this therapy might help her out and hopefully Mike could come alone so that they can see where they were going left in their relationship. Mike was thinking they had it all together, but something changed when he couldn't even help her prevent a possible bad situation from coming that could jeopardize their entire family.

6.
THE WEAPON IS TRYING TO FORM

Mateo couldn't wait to get back to his cousin's project so that he could see her again. Even though she showed signs that she clearly was going to be faithful to his cousin, he still thought that maybe there could be some kind of weakness in her, and that he could get her to break. He hoped that it wasn't too obvious during dinnertime with them, but he was so fascinated with her, and the only reason he wanted to come to dinner was because of her. He knew that his cousin was naive because he had always been that way even when they were growing up as kids. Mateo had become desperate to do whatever he needed to get close to her.

She on the other hand seemed to be a little more alert and that someone was going to have to be very smart to pull one over her head. He needed another plan to get him even closer to her, especially because the project was almost complete and there would be no other way to get close to her. How would he see her then? He thought about starting to follow her so that he could maybe see what her day would look like but thought that it would be too risky because she sometimes had her own security guard trailing her. The more he thought about a plan, the emptier he felt.

He decided that using his cousin would be the

33

best way because he knew that she was very submissive to her husband and that she would go along with whatever he decided to do. He decided to see if maybe he could come up with a lie about his house needing some renovations and that he needed a place to stay for a couple of days. It was a stretch, but he had to try because getting into the house would give him time to check out the house and maybe even to catch her in her most intimate times. He thought that he would call his cousin later to see if he would buy the lie so that he could execute his plan.

On the other hand, Layla had decided that she could meet with John now that she had his name and his place where he was born. John was good at his job and could find out about anyone if he wanted to. John told Layla to give him a few days and that he would let her know what he had found. Layla also asked John if he could get the camera footage from the panic room for the last two days because she wanted to see if anything seemed off. John let her know that it would be done and she would have both in a couple of days.

Layla could feel that the enemy was trying to form a weapon, but she knew in the word that God said it would form but it wouldn't prosper. Layla stood on the word of God and knew that if she kept God first, he would do the rest.

Mike went to work only to find that Jameelah was waiting in his office explaining to him that she needed someone to talk to; someone whom she could trust. She looked as if she had been crying all night pondering on something. She began to tell him that she and her fiancé after about five years were going their separate ways because of some disagreements they were having over her sexual desires.

Mike looked at her strangely and told her to stop right there. He called the lead administrator in the office and let her know that his coworker had some personal problems and that she needed to talk with someone. When his other female coworker came in, he immediately gave her some corrective action and let her know that she needed to only come to him for business matters and even with that she should be going to the manager of the administrators and not to him. He expressed to her that she was already out of line calling his home after business hours because he was happily married and didn't like any confusion. He also expressed to her that he had noticed that her outfits have gotten a little out of standard code and that she needed to review the handbook on the dress code for the company. He said that if she couldn't keep it business professional then maybe this company isn't where she needed to be. He then asked her if it was anything she needed clarity on or having any heartburn around?

Jameelah looked as if she was embarrassed and was about to cry. The manager of the administrators took over the conversation and then asked did she still have something she wanted to talk about? Jameelah declined to talk with her because she wanted to talk to Mike to see where he was with his marriage. She now knew where he stood and realized that if she didn't stop, she wouldn't have a job. She just couldn't stop thinking about him and where they could be if his wife was out of the picture.

She decided that she would get her act together so that she could at least see him every day but thought that maybe she should brainstorm some things to see if she could come up with something else. She was not one who would give up easily so she thought that maybe she could ask her play brother Mateo to help her with a plan because she knew that this was his cousin and he was much closer to Mike than she was.

Mateo was in his own thoughts when his phone rang. It was one of his closest friends. Jameelah and he were like brother and sister. One started a sentence and the other finished it. They had been friends for at least 20 years, and they could talk with each other about anything. They had both decided not to start a relationship because both of them came to the agreement that they would be like sister and brother and he didn't want to complicate their relationship. Mateo didn't have any brothers or sisters as he knew of because he didn't even get to meet his dad. His mother said that he had died, and he was too young to even know him. He was his mother's only child.

Jameelah and he went out together, used one another to get dates and even would lie for each other if it came down to it. When they were younger his friend had a very big crush on his cousin Mike, but he never looked her way. She was very attractive however Mike didn't seem to be interested in her. Jameelah had never gotten over that crush and she was very upset when she found out that Mike was getting married so fast to a girl that just came on the scene.

She overheard Mike talking to Mateo one night about needing another administrator at his company, so she asked Mateo to put a good word in for her. Mateo did just that and now she was working in his company. She also helped do payroll for Mateo's construction company because she had a good set of business skills from a degree she earned from college. She was a smart girl and even went back to get her master's in business management, minoring in Accounting.

Mateo and Jameelah were on the phone, and she said that she wanted to talk with him in person about what happened at the job today. Mateo decided to pick up some Chinese food and be ready for her when she came. It didn't take her long at all and in about fifteen minutes she was at the door.

She came in and got comfortable like she always did and immediately started telling him about the corrections she received from Mike and the manager over her department. She mentioned that she tried to see if his cousin was as faithful to his wife as he seemed by trying to hint at a conversation around being intimate with someone else. She told him that he corrected her and told her that she needed to revisit the company's handbook around dress code and that going forward she needed to go to her manager and not him.

Mateo was listening to her but formulating a plan that could help them both because he wanted his cousin's wife bad and he knew that she wanted Mike just as bad. He decided to talk with her about coming up with a plan that would work for both of them, to get what they both wanted.

He told her about the advancement that he tried to make on his cousin's wife and that she cut him off real fast and warned him that if he wasn't about business then he would be off the job. He also told her that he came to dinner that same night and she was very uncomfortable with it, and she even left them there to finish, while she went upstairs with her daughter to go to bed early. Jameelah listened and was also thinking of what they could do and realized that this could work in both of their favors. Both were more alike than they thought even down to wanting part of the same couple. They kept planning like two snakes in the grass and trying to see how and what they could do to tear a good relationship apart for their own benefits.

After about two hours later, Jameelah and Mateo had a plan that they would try to see how it played out. Mateo told Jameelah to do what she was told because he needed to keep her on the inside with his cousin. In the meantime, he would start seeing how he could get her to start finding ways so that they could start following them a little more to get any leverage they could on them both to use for their benefit. Jameelah agreed with the plan and even mentioned trying to get access to his computer so they might make him look like he was being unfaithful to cause problems at home and then maybe Mateo could step in at her weak point. She mentioned that women were weak when it is not working out at home and then it is possible that she would be vulnerable to his advances.

Both of them liked the plan and said that they

should start and keep each other in the loop of how the progress was going. Jameelah left and mentioned that she would watch more closely at work and needed to leave so she would not get home too late because she had to work in the morning.

They said their goodbyes and Jameelah left satisfied that she was going to one day get what she wanted and help her friend do the same thing. Mateo went to sleep thinking about how pretty Layla was and how she one day would be his no matter what the cost. He knew why his cousin was in love with her because it was something about her that made him feel different inside. He didn't know what it was, but it was a connection that he had never had with any other woman before in his life.

7.
COMMUNICATION IS ALWAYS THE KEY

It was starting to get late in the evening and Layla realized that she wasn't herself because she felt like something was changing and that she couldn't communicate with her husband. Layla was always comfortable telling her husband everything about her not leaving any details out, but lately she noticed that Mike had not been on her side, and it was starting to make her feel that something else was going on. She had been thinking about that dream since she had it the other night and realized that they didn't get to communicate about it for long. She was wondering how the coworker had been acting at work.

She was also thinking about her husband's cousin and whether she should just deal with him or not for her husband's sake but realized that it would be hard, especially how she saw him looking at her at dinner table the other night.

She decided to just wait until John gave her the information and then she could decide whether to deal with him or not. She didn't want to feel like she was going back into her shell after the situation happened to her, but she felt that more panic attacks were happening, and this situation felt like the other one that happened two years ago. She decided to give that therapist a call to see if she could come in sooner than later because she needed to start dealing with it as soon as possible.

Layla was deep in thought, and she hadn't realized that her husband was walking in the house towards the panic room to see how the project was coming along. Mateo and his team weren't on site today because they had to be somewhere else, so she guessed that Mateo had already told her husband about it. Mikaela and the maid were there watching a movie and eating snacks so that she could get some time for herself. She figured that she would see whether she needed to take over.

Layla walked in and her daughter was sleeping on her chair with her snack in her hand. Layla loved to see how beautiful her daughter was, especially when she was asleep. Layla eased the snack out of her daughter's hand and picked her up to take her upstairs to her room. When she turned towards the door her husband was standing in her walkway. He kissed her on the forehead, took his daughter from her arms and carried her up the stairs to her room.

Layla decided to ensure her husband didn't need anything like a bath, clothing or a plate fixed in the meantime. Mike said that he could use a relaxing bath because he wanted to talk to her about the day he had at work. Layla decided to run the bath for him and turn on the jets of the jacuzzi so that he could really relax. She planned to sit in the bathroom with him and even help bathe him so that they could spend quality time while they were talking.

Mike came into the room and immediately started telling her about the administrator at the job. Layla was quiet and let him do the talking while she listened and was washing his back. He began to tell her that she was right about bringing another person in if they had to talk because the girl had her own hidden agenda. He then began to tell her about the conversation that she was trying to have about a boyfriend and their sex lives and that he stopped her and brought in the female administrator to be a witness of the correction that he had to give to her.

Layla shook her head and realized that her dream was warning her about the enemy trying to come in between their relationship. She was wondering in her mind why her husband couldn't see what Mateo was trying to do but decided to let this be his moment and that they would talk about it later.

Layla was deep in thought when she heard Mateo's name from her husband's mouth. She came back to reality and asked him to repeat the last thing he had said. Mike told her that Mateo knew Jameelah and made an introduction to him about how good she would be at the company. He mentioned that she had a master's degree in Accounting and Administration and that she would be able to do the job very well.

Layla was in shock when she realized that the two snakes knew each other and now her mind was wondering whether they were working together to try to bring their relationship to an end. Layla decided that now was the best time to stay on the subject, so she asked her husband is it not weird that he is trying to make moves on her at the same time Jameelah was trying to make moves on him? Mike looked as if he saw a ghost. He turned to Layla and immediately started to take his cousin's side again.

Layla told him to not count out her theory, but it would be good to look more into it. She asked her husband if he knew how long his cousin knew this girl? Mike couldn't give a straight answer but the way he was fumbling over his words she realized that he may have known this girl before meeting her.

Layla left it alone and asked if they could pray so that they could have some clarity about what was going on. Mike agreed that prayer was needed and that it would help with the situation. They prayed together and decided to get some much-needed rest and talk about it later tomorrow. It didn't take long for both of them to fall off in a peaceful sleep where Layla was dreaming that they were on a beautiful island enjoying each other's company. The island was peaceful and the dream showed how their relationship was before there was a daughter and before all of the drama that was happening right now.

8.
TIME TO DEAL WITH SELF

Layla woke up to sunshine in her face and Mike standing over her already dressed for work. Layla rolled over in panic and realized that it was already after 8AM. She heard her daughter downstairs with the maid. She looked and Mike told her that he had already got her dressed for school and that she needed the rest, so he handled it for her.

Layla smiled at her husband and appreciated the man that God had given her. She would do whatever it took to be the best wife to him because he deserved it all. She let Mike know that she had to meet with the counselor today again and that she could have lunch with him afterwards.

Mike was glad about the idea and said that he would block his schedule for two hours so that they could leave the office and catch the breeze outside. She was overjoyed that she would get to spend some alone time with him outside the office.

Layla got up and started to get dressed so that she could run a couple of errands before the appointment. Mike let Layla know that the job would be finished by the end of the day in the panic room so the team would be working hard all day today. Layla said okay and that she would stay out long as she could because she wasn't that comfortable with his cousin.

Mike seemed to be a little bothered but didn't want to have an argument about it. Layla was happy that he would be done with the project and wouldn't have to be in her personal space anymore so she would just try to let it go.

Layla put on a pretty dress and some heels and went downstairs so that she could get a little breakfast before starting her day. Her daughter was singing loud and eating her oatmeal so Layla thought that she would join in and sing with her. Her daughter gave her the biggest hug and asked, was daddy taking her to school today?

Mike came in and answered her question before she could and agreed to take her to school on the way to work so that momma could eat her breakfast. Michaela was happy and said that she was ready to go now. Mike and their little girl gave Layla some love and sugar and said goodbye while walking out of the door.

Layla was talking to their maid when there was a ringing of the doorbell. The maid opened the door and Mateo's team started to head to the panic room to finish the project. Layla was about to go out the side door to her car when the security guard asked her to wait on him. She was waiting on the security team when Mateo walked in the door staring at her like he wanted or needed something from her. Layla gave him a disgusted look and told the security guard that she would be waiting in her car. She felt that her chest was tightening and that she was about to have another panic attack. She was confused about why this was happening because she thought they went away after the incident from last year! She knew that it was something else about him because she just had a good feeling in her heart. She also felt that her dreams were warning her so she would always keep her eyes open. She got her breathing under control and drank a bottle of water she had left in her car.

Mateo watched Layla from the back of the house and how she seemed to be having trouble with her breathing. He immediately felt that she was having feelings for him, and this was why he couldn't give up on her yet. He wanted to help her but knew that it was too risky, especially when he saw that the security guard was also going alone with her.

He had never felt like this with no other woman, and he knew why his cousin was crazy over her. Mateo had always been jealous of his cousin's life because he had everything given to him. He had a wonderful mother and an outstanding father. They had all the money you could ever want. They all had successful businesses and degrees and now he had the most beautiful wife you could imagine. He and his friend needed to work on their plan fast before his cousin finds out what he was really up to.

Layla did all her errands including getting a couple of things she needed from the store and thought it would be wise if she could try to beat traffic to make it to her appointment on the other side of town. Layla knew that she needed to see this counselor to start working on herself, but she was nervous on how it was going to go.

She walked into the office and checked in at the front desk. The receptionist let her know that Dianna was running a little behind but would be right with her. Layla said that it was fine and that she was grateful that Dianna was able to fit her in on short notice. Layla sat and was watching tv when she realized that the closed door was open and the therapist was showing her client out the front door.

Layla got nervous because she was up next, however, the nervousness was also excitement that she would have someone who would listen to her and not judge her. Layla's thoughts were interrupted by Dianna telling her welcome, and let's go to the office and get more comfortable.

The office was very cozy and relaxed. She had two long chairs with a coffee table in the middle. She was playing relaxing jazz music which complimented the candles and waterfall that she had on the table. The pictures were so beautiful and it put you in the mind of your favorite vacation spot at the beach. There was a pleasant aroma in the air that smelled of eucalyptus and lavender which was very relaxing.

Dianna began by asking about her daughter and how was her sleeping going? Layla told her that she hadn't woken up last night and it seemed better. Layla let the therapist know that when her daughter plays more and stays up a little longer she sleeps all night. The therapist then shifted the questions to her. How are you sleeping? Layla told her about her sleep and that sometimes she still has some bad dreams. Layla also told her about the panic attacks coming back since her husband's cousin has been doing work on the house.

The therapist listened and took her notes and continued to ask more questions, which started to pull the layers from Layla. She didn't realize that they had been talking over an hour and that she had updated Dianna on her attack last year, how she had been feeling that she was unable to talk to her husband about his cousin who had made a move on her and now she had started having bad dreams and anxiety around being stalked again.

Dianna informed her that this would take time and that she just must be able to put faith over fear, and that it was all an attack from the enemy who has no power at all. Dianna gave Layla ways to approach her husband on some things and that it would be good if they could come together sometimes. Layla said that she would mention it again but as for now she needed this time whether he wanted to come or not. They had to start ending the session but not before they prayed out so that they both could have strength to deal with the rest of their day. They set another appointment for later in the week and Layla left so that she could meet her husband for lunch.

Layla went to the other side of town to her husband's job stopping by Dewey's Bakery on the way. She picked up some cake squares so that her husband could have one of his favorite desserts for later. She got to the job about 12PM on the dot and went inside.

She was getting on the elevator when Jameelah hopped on with her. Layla spoke to her, but Jameelah didn't speak back. Layla stood in the middle while the girl stood in the back of her grilling her from the back. Layla was getting very heated and was trying to keep Jesus in her heart. Layla was not the one to take disrespect from anyone and especially not from a snake who wanted to be with her man.

Layla looked at her and asked her if she had a problem with her and if so, deal with it like an adult. Jameelah was about to try to say something smart when she realized that Layla could make her ruin the plan that her and Mateo had by getting fired. She looked at Layla with a fake grin and said, "Of course not, Mrs. Keaton. You have a great day." She got off the floor and went into her office. Layla got off on Mike's floor and was greeted by his assistant. "Mrs. Keaton, Mr. Keaton is expecting you in his office."

Layla said thank you and went into her husband's office. When she walked in her husband seemed to be in a serious conversation, however he recognized her and let her know that he was finishing up.

The time he was on the phone gave Layla time to just sit and admire her husband and recognize all the reasons she had fallen for him in the first place. She admired the way he knew how to be the boss and to be respectful to everyone that he was managing. He was just as attractive when she first saw him in her job when she was 17 years old and knew that even though he was older than she was she wanted to be his wife. He had been all she wanted and needed from a man and that's why she made her vows in front of God that she served and would honor them until the day she went to be with the Lord.

Mike got off the phone call and directed Layla to come and sit on his lap. Sometimes Mike would still treat Layla like she was his daughter because he wanted to always be the one to spoil her and give her what she needed. He began to ask her how her day went, and Layla was able to fill him in on how it went at the therapy session today.

He seemed to be very proud of her that she was working on herself and knew deep down he needed to be with her as well. Mike had seen a slight change in their relationship where his wife and him weren't as intimate with each other as they used to be. He realized that his daughter took up a lot of their time and thought about maybe taking a trip so that they could have some alone time with each other. He thought that he would get his assistant to start planning a trip so that they could get away from the everyday hustle and bustle and spend some quality time together.

Layla was just as beautiful to him as the first day that he saw her. He was still madly in love with her and would give his life for her. He knew that she wasn't happy with him when he stood up for his cousin instead of her, but he was always taught that family was first no matter what. He realized that she was his family now but at the time he didn't support her like he should have.

Mike had been in deep thought when he heard Jameelah's name come out of her mouth. Layla noticed that her husband was deep in thought about something, so she asked did he want to talk about it? Mike stayed on the subject and realized that he would rather go to lunch so that he could talk more about the conversation. Mike locked his computer and said there was a nice place that he wanted them to try in the downtown area.

Mike and Layla left the office and hopped in Mike's Bentley and were off to get some lunch. Mike was telling Layla how the office had been so busy lately and that they had a couple of big projects coming up soon. Mike's company was always busy doing different things for the city, so he stayed pretty busy at work. They pulled up to the place and the crowd looked relaxed, but it seemed to be really crowded.

Mike came around to open her door and they left the car for valet to park it. Mike gave the guy a tip and escorted his wife into the new place. Everyone knew who they were in the city so most of them just stared or nodded their heads to let them know they respected them. The manager came out to greet them because of who they were and to let them know that they would love the food here. The menu had soul food on it along with some great appetizers.

Mike and Layla decided to get an appetizer to share and then Mike ordered the filet mignon, baked potato and asparagus for both of them. The prices were a little expensive, however Mike cared about the quality more than the price. He mentioned that the place was supposed to be like Ruth's Chris Steak House, which had one of the best steaks they had ever tasted.

When the manager left, Mike dived in on how Jameelah had been acting kind of strange lately. He mentioned that she had been in his office lately acting like she had work to do but really didn't.

That conversation led Layla to tell him about her experience on the elevator and how disrespectful she was by not speaking back. Layla told Mike that she was trying to turn a new leaf, and that God provided a way for her to escape by the elevating stopping on the floor that they needed to go to because she was just about to give her a piece of her mind. Layla told her husband to be very careful because she has made it obvious that she wanted him more than just the boss and that she has no respect for him or him having a wife. Deep in both of their hearts they knew that she was a snake who would try to jeopardize their happiness for her.

The food was coming out and they really enjoyed the meal. They had some good conversations, including Mike apologizing for being insensitive to her needs when it came to his cousin. He even let her know that he would always support her and that he would be more observant with the situation.

Layla felt much better and knew that with them praying together more, God would make everything right again. Mike even agreed that he would attend some therapy sessions with her when she was ready but to make sure she worked around his schedule at work because he was busy. Layla let Mike know that she had his favorite dessert and they would spend more time together tonight.

The look on his face told Layla that he was

happy about that and that he had been missing her on that level. Layla realized that Mike may have been feeling neglected in that area, however she was tired after being a mother and a wife on a regular basis. She realized that with her getting more sleep she seemed a little better at being able to cater to her husband's needs so maybe everything was getting better.

Mike put a big tip on the table and let the valet know that he was ready for the car. The valet was back in a flash, and they were heading back towards the office. Layla felt like they had accomplished something today and needed to spend more time together. Mike and Layla pulled back up and Mike walked her to her car and ensured that she was safely in and let her know that he would see her back at home.

Layla jumped in her car and noticed that she still had a couple of hours before her daughter got out of school. She decided to go get a little workout before picking up her daughter. She grabbed her change of clothes which consisted of a pair of running shorts, a tank top and some comfortable shoes from the trunk and went to the track closest to her daughter's school. She was getting a good workout and thought that she would go get something to drink from the concession stand at the park that was connected to the track.

She was in the line when she thought that she heard a familiar voice. She looked towards the familiar voice and the voice led her to the picnic tables to see Mateo and her husband's administrator having a cordial conversation over some lunch. Something about the situation didn't seem right which made Layla want to get a little closer and listen to what they were saying,

Layla's breathing started getting a little heavier, so she decided that it was enough excitement for today. She thought that he had to finish up the panic room and here he was at the spot that she runs at. Was this a coincidence? Did she get followed here? Layla had too many questions and no answers, but she felt it was important to let her husband know that her suspicions may be right.

Layla was heading back toward her car when she heard Mateo call out her name. She turned around and noticed that he was admiring her in her workout clothes. He came closer and offered her an apology for trying to make a move on her at her home. He explained that he was out of line and that it wouldn't happen again.

Layla accepted his apology but still felt it was necessary to keep her eyes open. She looked back at the picnic tables and realized that Jameelah was no longer there. She was wondering if she was still in the park or had left. She let him know that she accepted his apology but let him know that she had to leave to go and pick up her daughter.

Layla was almost to her car when she realized that her tire was completely flat. She didn't have any issues with her tires and didn't understand why one was already flat.

Mateo sat back and watched their plan come into motion. He had Jameelah put a tracking device on her car while Mike and her were at lunch today. This plan led to him sitting outside the job and following her to the next destination. He was glad to see that she wasn't going home but when she pulled up at the park he called Jameelah to meet him at the park so that they could work out another plan. The plan worked faster than they thought when she came to get something to drink. Jameelah decided that if she flats the tire then it will force her to be with him a little more longer.

Layla was on the phone calling her husband to pick up their daughter on time from school because she was going to wait for Triple A to come but that's when Mateo came up behind her and asked her if she had a spare? Mike immediately knew his cousin's voice and asked his wife to put him on the phone. Layla handed the phone to Mateo, and she could hear her husband asking him to watch over her and to change the tire for her so she wouldn't have to wait a long time for insurance to send someone.

Layla was very frustrated that her husband was so naive. Layla didn't want to sound ungrateful, but she could have accepted help from any other man but him. Her husband got back on the phone with her, and he let her know of the decisions that he had made in the situation. Layla decided that it wasn't much she could do right now, so she got in the trunk, showed him where the spare was and handed him what he needed to get started.

Mateo knew that she was upset but she was gorgeous when she was mad. He had to control his emotions and be the person he needed to be for her right now, which was the mechanic. It took him about forty-five minutes to change the tire. It felt like it was an eternity because Layla knew that she would want to be with anyone else but him.

After he had finished changing the tire he apologized again for making her feel uncomfortable but wanted to know if they could start over. Layla had a very uneasy feeling in her stomach and so she said that she had to leave. Layla got in her car and left Mateo standing there looking confused and thinking about what his next move was.

Layla got home and heard her husband and her daughter in the kitchen. Layla darted up the stairs and decided that she needed to really get herself together. She was having mixed feelings right now. Her husband and she had just had a wonderful lunch and a good understanding about getting back on track with everything. Why would her husband not be considerate again, or was she overreacting and should have tried to put everything into the past? She couldn't get her thoughts together.

Mike walked up behind her, and she jumped out of her skin. She screamed but when she realized that it was her husband, she felt so embarrassed. Mike realized that this was out of his wife's normal, so he thought they needed to talk about it.

Layla was on the verge of having a panic attack but was able to calm down when it was Mike. Mike let Layla know that their daughter was in her playroom watching her favorite shows with the maid and that they should talk about it.

Layla told Mike that she went by the park to get

her work out on, and that Mateo and his administrator Jameelah were in the park together. Layla told him that it was mysterious that Jameelah was there one minute and gone the next while Mateo was trying to apologize for trying to make a move on her and that he wanted their relationship to start over.

Layla told her husband that she felt that something was not right with both of them and that she felts that they were working together for a common goal. She also let her husband know that the tire should have never been flat and that she felt that someone did it intentionally like Jameelah. She knew that Jameelah wanted revenge, but she had gone too far.

Mike said that he believed her and that he would talk with his connections to see if he could get any camera shots of what happened in the park and that he would get John involved if needed be. Layla knew that her gut feeling was correct, but it reminded her to talk with John to see what he was able to find out with the camera footage from the house on the day that he tried to make a move on her and what he was able to find out about the history of the mysterious Mateo.

9.
DON'T PERISH FOR A LACK OF KNOWLEDGE

Layla woke up feeling very tired as if she hadn't slept at all the night before. She laid in bed and thought about the events that had happened yesterday and realized that she needed to put on her investigator's hat and find out a little more on what they were up against.

Mike and her daughter were already downstairs in the kitchen spending their quality time and eating breakfast. Mike had gotten up and did her morning motherhood duties so that she could sleep in again. She reminded herself to thank him for that because he was really giving her a much-needed break.

Layla went into the bathroom to get dressed and decided on some comfortable clothes because she knew that she had to take care of some small projects around the house. She had planned to take her daughter to school and then get rid of some clothes that her daughter needed to donate and then clean her daughter's playroom up so that it would be clean from germs. Layla put on an all-over one-piece workout pants suit and some tennis shoes with some earrings and a necklace. She was pretty in everything she wore so even on a bad day it was still looking like she was a model from *Jet* magazine.

Layla went downstairs to spend some time with

her family before everyone got gone and her husband gave her a look that let her know that he liked what he saw. Layla smiled and kissed him and picked her daughter up from the table. Mike kept his eyes on his wife admiring how he was the luckiest man in the world to have a woman so beautiful. Even after having his child, she was still in tip-top shape and could still be an outstanding model. Mike realized that her mother and her sisters all had great genes and were all so beautiful like their mother Cindy.

His cousins would have been crazy not to try to get with her sisters because they were not just beautiful but confident and strong. None of them seemed to be aging at all and their ages would be very hard to guess.

Mike was in his own world thinking about how he was going to get his wife away so that he could have her all to himself when Layla interrupted his thoughts by asking who was taking Michaela to school today? Mike said that he would take her on his way to work and that she could go on with her day. Layla told him that she had some things to do around the house and if he needed her to bring him lunch today.

Mike told her not to worry about it because he was going to try to meet up with Mateo to get to the bottom of what was going on. Layla told him to be careful and that if anything changes to let her know. Mike and Michaela were leaving out the door and securing the home.

Layla went up to John's office and knocked on the door. John told her to come in because he could see her from the cameras. John was so good at his job. If you wanted any information, he could get it and he had a set of military skills that you didn't want to play with. John was getting the footage of the tape that she had requested. John was pulling it up on the big screens so that she could watch the house at the time when Mateo tried to make a move on her.

She went back and watched, and she noticed that Mateo wasn't doing any panic room work at all. His team had covered it and the only work he was doing was watching her. She noticed that he could watch her from the back part of the house and knew when she was coming and going. John was letting her know that Mateo must have known where all the cameras were because the camera didn't capture him making a move on her because of where they were standing.

Layla was a little upset when she didn't have the actual proof, however John showed her a little after everything had happened. Layla was in the playroom with her daughter and John was able to capture Mateo coming into the house and watching her for about five minutes while her daughter and she were in the playroom.

John told Layla that Mateo knew the house but was bold enough to watch her because the maid and butler were in another part of the house. He mentioned that she never paid any attention to him and that she needed to be careful. He then started showing Layla his family history and that he found out that his daddy had been deceased for a while. His daddy was named Woodrow Rankins, and he seemed to be much older in age when he had Mateo.

Layla's breathing started to get faster because she knew that name from somewhere. John let Layla know that Woodrow Rankins was married to a lady who died due to an overdose and that she was believed to be a prostitute. He had other children, which meant that Mateo possibly had brothers and sisters. This sounded too familiar to Layla, but she tried to calm down so that she could hear it to the end.

John then mentioned what she believed to be one of her worst fears. He mentioned that he had a son who had done some bad crimes involving kidnapping and sexual assault and that he died mysteriously in prison. Layla fainted right on the floor.

When she woke up the ambulance and Mike were at her side and to her surprise her mother was in the area and got there as soon as she heard.

Layla was so embarrassed. She noticed that she had some blood on her arm and a massive headache. She must have hit her head because the paramedics were asking her questions to test her memory. John and Mike were talking about what happened before she passed out and a look of shock was on his face.

Mike came to hold his wife in his arms while apologizing for not looking more into it sooner. John must have spoken to him on how Mateo had been trying to make his move on to his wife but he was too blind to see it. Mike had no idea who Mateo's father was but now it made perfect sense that Mateo was the brother to Wilson who was the sick individual who had been stalking his wife, confessed to killing a cop and a young girl, took her hostage and went to prison for it.

He knew that Mateo's mother which was the sister to his mother came up on a different side of life and that she was a stripper and got pregnant by an older man, but he would have never known that she had gotten pregnant by the man who possibly got off on killing his wife and had a sick son who was following in his footsteps because he was a damaged kid that would see what was going on with his father. It was a small world to know that even Layla's mother would take rides with him because she didn't drive and he was the main person that would take her on her errands. This was a man who was very sick and loved to have control over women.

Mike knew that God existed because Layla's mother could have easily been a victim and her girls as well. If that had happened, he would never have been blessed with his soulmate and a beautiful daughter.

Mike constantly apologized to his wife for not seeing her side and that he was trying to keep from having hate for his cousin Mateo. Mateo was trying to get what he had. The more he thought about it the more his childhood came back, and that Mateo was always jealous of him because of what he had. His cousin wanted everything he had, even the girls he was dating.

Mateo knew that Mike was trying to talk with those girls, but he would still try to get with them anyway. He thought that it was a sibling rivalry type thing and that it would go away when they got older, but he saw now that it never did. Now that he knew what was really going on he was sure to make John move faster on getting video surveillance of the park because it was mighty strange that Mateo happened to be at the same park his wife was at on the same day and at the same time. He also needed to see who Jameelah really was and why Mateo and she were so close.

Mike had a lot that he needed to do at home, so he had already decided that he needed to take some days off to take care of home fires. Mike let his wife know that she was going to be okay and that once everything got back to normal, she needed to keep talking with her therapist.

Layla let him know that she was already scheduled for another one next week. He also let her know that he would be out of work for a little while because he needed to get some things in order at home. He would be working from home if needed be and he would let his assistant know that she could call if she needed him to handle anything important. Mike had so many things on his mind and John was already on it making sure the house wasn't bugged and checking the cars for bugs.

The paramedics cleared Layla from any head injuries or major injuries but said that she needed to get plenty of rest and drink plenty of fluids. Mike let them know that she would be taken care of and that they would do what was instructed by the medical professionals.

When the paramedics left, Layla looked at Mike with a silent apology and Mike grabbed her and looked her in the eyes to let her know that she didn't have to worry about anything. Her mother was very supportive and let her know that she would be getting some clothes and staying in the mansion for a while to spend some time with her family and granddaughter. Layla had a big smile on her face because she knew when mom was there, she would be alright.

Mike was glad to hear that her mother would be staying a while, which would give him time to handle some outside business with John and Mateo. Her mother said that she was going to pick up Michaela early and spend some time with her and that it probably would be best if they all stayed in the mansion until this situation ended.

Mike agreed but let them know that if they were needing to go somewhere that a member of the security team needed to always be with them. Layla thought it would be best if her mother drove her car since the car seat was already in it and she wouldn't have to change things around. Her mother said that would be fine. Her mother got the spare keys and left and locked the door behind herself.

Mike and Layla were talking silently when Layla told Mike that the camera footage didn't show where he actually tried to make a move on her, but it did show that he had been watching her in the house. Mike let her know that he believed her and knew everything because John filled him in. He also let her know that John had the video footage from the park because she had done well with parking her car in the view of a camera in the park. Layla was happy to hear that and knew that John would get what they needed.

John had already had a meeting with the security

team showing them the pictures of Mateo and letting them know that he was not welcome anywhere near the property and to contact the authorities because they didn't know what his intentions were.

Layla went into the kitchen to the medicine cabinet to get something for her headache. She got a bottle of water and took two Tylenols and laid back on the living chair with her head in Mike's lap. Mike couldn't control his thoughts of how his cousin was again trying to take what was his.

Layla sensed tension while laying on Mike and got in his lap to comfort him and prayed for him. She let him know that God would fight their battles and that everything would be ok. He was glad that Layla always stayed trying to do things right by God which is why they were so blessed. Layla let Mike know when everything got back to normal that she would love to take a trip with him so that they could spend some much-needed quality time.

Mike agreed but didn't tell her that he had already planned for them to be gone next month so that they could spend time together. His mother wanted Michaela for the whole month, so he planned to have his wife all to himself.

Mike's phone was ringing, and it was John. Layla listened as John told Mike that her tire was flattened by a girl in the park. Mike said that he was sending the video footage to his phone. Mike put the phone on speaker so that Layla could hear and he pulled the picture of the girl in the park up to see who had caused the damage. When the picture came up Layla recognized the outfit and the girl who was Jameelah.

The camera captured how Mateo was watching Layla on the phone at the park which was when she was talking to him which clarified that this was planned from the get-go. Mike was furious. He thanked John and John also said that he didn't find any bugs in the house, or in Mike's car but he wasn't able to check Layla's car because her mother had it.

Mike thanked him for being on it and let him know that he was about to call his second in command to let Jameelah go for the evidence that they now had. Mike knew that Jameelah was giving signals, but he never thought that she would do something like this to his wife. She had to go, and charges must be pressed on her for trying to destroy his wife.

Mike and Layla talked for a little about the evidence that was discovered, however, Layla said that Mike should let her go from the company and not ruin the company's image, but don't press charges on her for the car.

Mike let Layla know that the police needed to know as well so they agreed that maybe doing a restraining order on her and Mateo would be wise. Mike called his company and asked if Jameelah was at work today. His administrator said that Jameelah had left early today, and she had put her two weeks in due to dealing with a family emergency and that she would be moving to another state.

Mike knew that this was strange and let his administrator know that he was coming in so that they could have a meeting with all the employees in the

Human Resource department. Mike let his second in command deactivate her key card so that she wouldn't be able to come back in and to have the security check to make sure that she was not still in the building. He was also instructed to check her office and pack all her things up for her neatly and to ensure that her computer was wiped clean of all business related to their company and to deactivate her internet and passwords as well. She let Mike know that she would be on it and she understood that this was a priority.

Mike hung up with her and decided to let Layla know that he wanted her to come with him to the office because he didn't want to leave her alone, but he needed to handle this asap. Layla agreed to come and didn't want to be left alone at the mansion. Layla was glad that now that they knew what was going on that they could put a plan in place to keep everyone safe.

10.
WE KNOW WHO THE ENEMIES ARE

Layla and Mike arrived at the office about 30 minutes later to get their business in order. When Mike arrived, he went to his office and checked his computer for any viruses or anything that may not look right. He walked around checking his office for any bugs or cameras that shouldn't be there. His second in command was already coming towards the office to let Mike know that everyone was already in the conference room waiting on him.

Mike and Layla headed towards the conference room which was on the floor up from Mike's office. They got into the elevator and went one floor up. They were walking towards the conference room when Mike said that he had felt a pull in his chest and a little tingling in his left shoulder. Layla asked him if he was ok, or did he need to go check on it but Mike said that he would be fine and that he would go when things got back on the right track. Layla knew that meant that he wasn't going to check on it but she would remind him a little later.

Everyone spoke to them when they entered and some of the employees were glad to see Layla and asked how their pretty little girl was doing. Layla loved Mike's employees because they had so much respect towards them. Mike let them catch up for a while and

68

then he jumped right into business. He let them know about the incident of Jameelah calling his house very late at night pretending to have business to talk about which she was reprimanded for. He also let them know how she had tried to have an inappropriate conversation with him, which he brought the manager in to witness him giving her a second reprimand and also told her that if she couldn't represent this business professionally then maybe she should look for another job. He also told the company that he had seen her in his office a couple of times but didn't know why she was there. He mentioned that it had been discovered that she may be working with his cousin for their own personal agendas to ruin his marriage.

Layla chimed in and told her how disrespectful Jameelah was to her on the elevator and how they had gotten video coverage that Mike's cousin and she knew each other and worked together to get her stranded at the park by Jameelah who flattened her tire.

Mike also let the company know that Mateo, his cousin, had been doing some work at the house and had tried to make a move on his wife and now they have reasons to believe that they could be dangerous. Mike let the company know that safety was first and this is why Jameelah will not be working out her last two weeks. Human resources needed to go ahead and pay her for the two weeks but let her know that she doesn't need to come back because of the restraining order that will be placed. If she comes back anywhere around the business or anywhere near either one of them, they will involve the authorities.

Everyone agreed that this would be the best and that it is best that no one from the company try to have any contact with her but the HR team. Mike let them know that, right now, they have to play it safe because they don't know what her next move may be. Mike asked if there were any questions or concerns and everybody seemed to know what part they had to play in ensuring that everyone was safe.

The HR team said that they would call her and let her know how this would work and that her items would be mailed to her address. They would also let her know that she would get paid even though she wouldn't be working her last two weeks. The meeting was over and everyone went back into their work modes.

Mike thought he would ensure that everything was locked up in his office and get his computer packed up so that he could have access to work while he was at home making sure everything was being handled to his standards.

Mike had a lot on his mind because now that these new events had transpired, he didn't know what his cousin and his friend's next moves could be. He decided to give John a call to have him check on her background to see who she really was. He never thought that his cousin would send a snake to his company but knowing whose son he belonged to he wasn't going to assume anything else.

Layla was watching her husband in all his thoughts and was wondering how she could help him with dealing with these types of situations. She wanted to be supportive, but she also didn't want to overstep her boundaries in his workplace. She decided to just pray and stand in the gap for her husband in silence. Mike had packed his laptop up and put some paperwork in his work bag and was heading towards the door when Layla realized that they were about to leave. Mike said his goodbyes to his coworkers and the coworkers let him know that he didn't have to worry, that everyone was on their game and the company would be fine.

Layla and Mike went to the elevator and Mike pushed the down button and headed towards the basement. When the elevator got down to the basement Mike decided to stop by the security booth to ensure that they were also on their A-game. He couldn't afford any protocols being breached and he wanted to ensure that all of his employees would be safe at work and at home.

Mike was talking with the security team, and everyone was already aware of what was going on and they had made it clear that her badge was inactive and she would not be able to enter the building. They also let Mike know that they had done a detailed search of the building and she was not in the building. Mike felt better and let them know that if anything happens, they need to call him so that he would be able to stay in the loop of things. Mike and Layla left and walked towards Mike's parking spot in the basement while security was watching.

11.
WHAT IS DONE IN THE DARK
WILL COME TO THE LIGHT

Layla and Mike were riding home and talking about whether there were things that Layla needed to pick up from the store or was she going to call and place an order online? Layla didn't think that she might need to go to the store because her mother was here and loved to cook in the kitchen. Layla was excited that her mother would cook her some of that good soul food that she was raised on, and it would be just like old times.

Layla let Mike know that she would do an online order to give her mom some time to get involved with making the list. He agreed and realized that it was still early in the day and that he and Layla had some time alone since Layla's mother was getting their daughter from school.

Mike started to think that he could really use some intimate time with his wife, but he didn't want to be insensitive to all the events that had just happened today. He decided that he would give her some time to process it all but maybe hint on it a little later.

He was about to at least take her to get some ice cream when his phone rang and it was one of the security guards from the house who was following Layla's mother. Mike answered the phone, and the security guard was letting Mike know that it was a suspicious vehicle following Layla's car that her mother was in and if he should act or not.

Layla overheard the conversation and was wondering if her daughter was in the car. The security guard said that she was safe and driving towards the park area. Mike asked for the location and Layla was already on the phone calling her mother to let her know to keep driving and not stop anywhere because she was possibly being followed, however the security guard was with her and handling it.

Mike started to get angry and after asking the guard to send his location to his iPhone so that he could see who this person was. He realized that this person had to think that Layla's mother was Layla because it was his wife's car that was being followed.

The location was about ten minutes away, which was enough time to talk about the plan. Layla and Mike were already ready for whatever. Layla didn't play any games when it came to her family, especially her daughter and her mother. Layla was already dressed to get in the boxing ring if she had to, but she knew that Mike probably wouldn't let her.

In no time they had reached the location and were following the security guard. Layla and Mike could see what the car looked like, and it wasn't one that she saw Mateo drive. It was a black pickup truck with North Carolina's tags on it. The driver was a male but neither of them could see any of the features from the back. Layla called her mother and told her mother to pull over at the next store but to stay in the car with the doors locked.

Tamelia Keaton

Layla's mother did as she was instructed, however everyone else followed suit. The mysterious car pulled over to the other side of the gas station as if he needed to get gas as well. He hadn't noticed that there was a security guard driving a regular Honda Accord who had been also following the car and trailing him as well. Mike and Layla had pulled up to the other side of the gas station so that the mysterious man wouldn't get suspicious.

The mysterious man got out of the car so he wouldn't look suspicious, and the guard and Mike did the same. The guy was wearing all black with black sunglasses and a baseball cap which was clearly a disguise. The guy got a soda and a candy bar and went up to pay for his items while watching to see what was going on in the car he had followed.

The cashier asked him if he needed anything else and the mysterious guy spoke. Mike immediately knew his cousin's voice and anger boiled up in his chest. The guard sensed that Mike was upset and came to his side. He waited until his cousin went back to the suspicious car and followed him.

When he got outside, he called his cousin's name, and the mysterious man answered his identity. Mike confronted him and asked what he was doing in this area. Mateo knew that he was caught. He looked in the car and realized that it wasn't Layla in the car he was following but a lady who looked to be an older version of her, meaning it was probably her mother.

Layla was waiting impatiently in the car when she couldn't wait any longer. Mike hadn't come back

74

yet, and she needed to know if everyone was okay. Layla got out of the car and went into the store. When she didn't see anyone, she immediately went out towards where her car was parked and that is when she looked towards her husband and a man talking to each other. She couldn't see who the guy was because he seemed to be in disguise, so she got in the car with her mother and daughter.

Mateo saw Layla walking towards the car to get in with her mother and daughter and he couldn't help but put all his focus on her. He was upset that he was caught and now he wouldn't be able to get out of this one with his cousin. Mike confronted his cousin and let him know that he knew what he was up to. Mike and Mateo got into a heated argument and the security guard had already called the police.

Mateo pushed Mike and Mike swung and hit Mateo in the face. Mateo wasn't a push over and Layla got out of the car to try to help diffuse the situation. Mateo picked Mike up and slammed him on the cement. That was all he wrote. Before the security guard could interfere, Mike got on top and beat his cousin until he was almost unconscious.

Layla knew that Mike knew how to protect their family, but she didn't want either of them to get hurt as well. It wasn't long before it was a big crowd, cameras everywhere and police sirens in view. The police came and ensured that the fight was stopped and one of the police called the ambulance because Mike had blood on his head from hitting his head on the cement when Mateo slammed him, but Mateo's face was almost unrecognizable due to all the blood and scars on it.

The police officer was getting Mike's statement, and the guard was giving his statement of what was going on. Layla was also talking with the cop who was with Mike giving her statements about the events leading up to this one and Mateo was getting looked at by EMS. Another officer was also with Mateo by the ambulance trying to get his statement of what happened as well.

Mike and Mateo were both being asked if they would like to press charges, but both of them declined. Mike and Layla both were letting the officer know that they would like a restraining order on Mateo and that they were going to also do it for his friend Jameelah. The officer let them know that it would be a 50C instead since there was no relationship between either of them.

Mike was letting Layla know that he had a bad headache, but he refused to go to the doctor to see about the little gash that was on his head. He said that he would take some pain medicine and get some rest and if it persisted, he would check on it later.

Layla was filling her mother in on what they found out about Mateo's father and that his brother was Wilson. Her mother was very sorry and felt responsible for not believing her when she told her as a child about how she was uncomfortable around Woodrow when he was living. She had no idea that they were all related and that she had her girls in danger while riding with him before she was driving on her own.

Her mother let her know that she was going to

76

take Michaela home and feed her and lay her down for a nap and that she would start dinner after she got her granddaughter settled. Layla let her know that Mike and she would be home shortly after they finished up there.

Mike was finishing up with the police officer when he received a call from his mother. She had seen it on social media and wanted to make sure everyone was okay. Mike told his mother that Mateo and he had got into a fight because Mateo had made a move on his wife and Mateo and his friend Jameelah had crossed the line with putting his family in danger. His mother was so upset and was also making sure that Mateo was not hurt too badly. Mike assured her that he was ok and that he would always be family.

Mike's mother said that she knew Jameelah and knew that Jameelah used to like both Mateo and him when they were younger and that she always kept some mess started between both of them. Mike couldn't remember it too well because he wasn't interested in her but realized that she had been in his life for a long time. Mike started to realize that she was probably one of the angry women when he married Layla and just didn't pay it any attention.

Mike let his mother know that Cindy was here with them and that made his mother proud. She said that she would love to see Layla's mother and she knew that she would take great care of all of them in her absence. She said that she would take a trip, but Mike's daddy was under the weather, and she didn't want to leave him home alone. Mike understood and let his mother know that he was taking some days off and that they would come there real soon to visit. Mike told his mother that he loved her and that he would talk with her later.

12.
HAPPILY, EVER AFTER

Layla and Mike were at home having a great conversation about everything that had happened in the last couple of weeks. Layla was letting Mike know that they would always be a team, but they needed to pray about things together more so that God could give them discernment on situations like these.

Mike agreed and let Layla know that she was his rib for a reason and that he will always take her side, no matter who it is. He realized that he had made a big mistake by not believing his wife and that this situation could have been much worse. He agreed to start going to counseling with her and that he was willing to do whatever it took to keep his marriage in line with God.

Mike's company had found out that Jameelah was not who she said SHEwas. She had lied on her application about her credentials and just wanted to work close to Mike. She had left town knowing that this was not her first rodeo on trying to trap a rich businessman. Mike found out that she had been after him since high school and he had never given her the time of the day, so she gravitated to his cousin Mateo.

Mateo decided to move out of the state as well because he felt it would be the best way to ensure that he wouldn't see Layla and to get in trouble with the law again. Mike let Layla know that his parents wanted their daughter for a month and that he wanted to get away from home and possibly catch up on some much-needed quality time with his wife. Layla was very excited about that and agreed that it couldn't have came at a better time.

Mike and Layla decided to start packing for their trip early. Layla and Mike had gotten over a weapon that was formed by the enemy, but it didn't prosper in their marriage. Layla and Mike lived happily ever after and didn't let anybody come in between their marriage ever again, not even family.

THE END

STRUGGLES WITH THE HEALTH

It was a hot summer day and Lauren was just coming back in from helping her husband get some food off the grill. Lauren was blessed that she had a husband that could cook, clean and protect her if needed be. Lauren had a great husband named Jim who had been a soldier in the Army which caused him to be disciplined with everything even in the civilian world.

Jim had fought two wars for this country but had to be released because he was struck by lightning while he was on active duty. That didn't stop her husband; he was a man of God who had a goal to find him a couple of good soldiers who would fight to help lead more men to Christ. He believed in the Army's saying not to leave any man behind.

Lauren and Jim were very respected at their church and were looked at like the ideal couple. They were very involved with the church and knew that they had to always honor the Lord first no matter what. Jim was quite the gentleman and everyone around them knew that he would give Lauren the world if he could. He didn't miss an opportunity to always open the car doors for her and to always be her support in anything that she wanted to do in life.

Jim was romantic and knew how to always keep her wondering what he would do next when it came to holidays, anniversaries and things that were important to both of them. Lauren didn't like the outside much but loved it when her husband cooked on the grill, so she decided to assist him so that she could say that she helped.

The food was all done cooking on the grill which included steaks, mixed vegetables, hot dogs, chicken and corn on the cob. Lauren had made some potato salad, homemade baked beans and some homemade lemonade to go along with the grilled foods. They were about to eat good. They decided to watch a movie that they had saved for later so that they could continue to spend some quality time together. Lauren and Jim were serious about ensuring that they would get their quality time in no matter what came up. They were definitely each other's soul mate.

They had two boys who were young men now and both were attending college. One was studying Psychology and the other was studying Digital Media. This gave Lauren and Jim flexibility to go when they wanted to and enjoy each other's company more often without any interruptions. Lauren didn't work because her husband wanted her to be a housewife and to pursue her dreams of becoming a writer, so she took advantage of writing in her spare time and attending college, pursuing her master's degree in Psychology.

Jim did some private investigating work which bought in great money alone by adding with his 100 percent military disability which paid all the bills. They were not in need for anything, and God had blessed them and given them the desires of their heart and that is why they never missed a beat with paying their tithes and blessing their church and their leaders.

Lauren was fixing their plates when her husband said that he would like them to get out of town for Thanksgiving this year. He mentioned that he wanted to check out this resort in Wilmington, NC. Lauren was excited about the trip and said that she had wanted to check out that beach as well because she heard that it was very nice. They had decided that they would do it before Thanksgiving because he wanted to be home when the boys came back home from their break. Lauren loved that her husband always took the initiative to take control of their relationship because he always seemed to make the best decisions in everything he did.

Lauren was thinking about the fifteen years that they had been married and all the good and bad things that they had been through. Lauren realized that they had moved a lot of different times because of his duty stations changing often and how exciting it was to have experienced a lot of different states in the process.

She wasn't glad that her husband had to come out of the military due to a health challenge, but she was glad that she was able to stay in North Carolina. She loved that North Carolina gave you the experience of seeing all the seasons and that it was not a fast city. She had experienced New York and other States that seemed very fast paced while moving all the time.

North Carolina was more of the country and the people were nice there. The state didn't get a lot of snow, and the weather was great as well. Lauren thought it was funny that when they did get bad weather, the state would shut things down these and everyone would go to the store and buy all the bread, eggs and milk. Jim would make jokes that everyone obviously couldn't live without a soggy egg sandwich which would have Lauren laughing until she cried.

Lauren realized that her husband had so many great qualities of a real man, but one of his qualities that she didn't like was because he was a strong man he didn't seem to take care of his health like he should. Jim didn't go to the doctor on a regular basis like she did because he always said that he was ok and, in the military, they were trained to keep on moving no matter what and that it wasn't anything wrong with him that the Lord couldn't fix. She could count on her fingers how many times that her husband went to a hospital and you better believe, it had to be a dying emergency for him to go in the first place. Lauren even invited him to a couple of her appointments to see what it looks like to have a primary care physician and the benefits, but it still didn't encourage her husband to find one.

Lauren believed in taking care of her health and she even participated in Zumba two times a week at the MEC with the best Zumba instructor in the world. His name was Dwaine and Lauren was glad that he focused on Faith, Family and Fun. She had been trying to get her husband to attend some days, but he mentioned that Zumba was more geared to a woman sport and that he rather hit the gym and lift some weights.

Lauren noticed that her husband was eating more and not working out as much and had begun to gain some extra pounds. When Lauren mentioned his weight Jim would get very upset, so Layla decided to keep hinting at it here or there. She noticed that she cared about her husband's health more than he did and decided that she would leave it alone all together. Lauren noticed that they weren't getting any younger and she was already in her 40's and her husband was in his 50's and that things would start changing anyway. Lauren was just trying to be cautious because she knew that her husband's father and mother both died of heart attacks, so she wanted to have her husband as long as possible.

Lauren remembered that her mother had the same issue with her father who never wanted to go to the doctor and her mother made a comment that black men needed to do better with their health and go to the doctor on the regular! When her father decided to start going, he found out that he had high blood pressure and that he had prostate cancer which they were able to treat in time because it was discovered early enough. Even though her husband was fit on the outside and was well in shape she wanted to make sure that it was the same on the inside. Lauren just wanted an opportunity to have her husband for a long time period She trusted God and knew that life and death was in his power. She just wanted to ensure that they were doing their part while on earth.

Three Months Later....

Lauren was putting her last things in her suitcase to prepare for their planned trip when she received a phone call from her mother. Her mother was letting her know that her father had one last radiation treatment and that he was able to ring the bell which let them know that his cancer was not seen anymore and that it was in remission.

Lauren was very happy to hear it because her daddy had to go through weeks of radiation, and it was beginning to make her mother tired. Lauren would support by taking her daddy to some of his treatments so that her mother could do something else, even if it was to get some rest. Her father was starting to get grumpier in his older days and Lauren and he would get into many heated debates over different situations.

Lauren let her mother know that they should all celebrate when she and her husband got back from their trip. Her mother agreed and let her know that she wanted them to have fun on their trip and spending quality time alone with your husband in a different place helps with keeping the marriage fun and exciting.

Lauren heard Jim coming into the bedroom from his workout and so she told her mother that she loved her and that she would call them tomorrow when they got on the road. Jim loved the relationship that his wife had with her family. Jim had never heard of the sitting crew until he married his wife. Her mother had five sisters and three brothers and a lot of best friends who were like sisters. They would meet up at one of the family's houses and sit, talk, drink coffee and spend time just enjoying each other's company. It didn't matter how hot it was outside, if the sitting crew came to your house they were going to ask for coffee. They were strong women who didn't play any games with anybody. What came up always came out and some of the things that came out could cut you or have you laughing so hard that you couldn't stop.

They all were raised from a loveable woman who would give her last meal to anyone who needed more than she did. She went by the name of Coot and she raised her nine kids with love and the fear of God. When she was living, she loved a lot of company even if you were just there to sit and look at her, and when she passed the traditions passed on and all her children could cook just like her which was some good old soul food cooking.

They were all from the South and knew how to make a meal out of what they had which gave them good survivor skills. The women were very strong and would work to take care of themselves. On the other hand, because the three boys were the babies, they weren't as independent as the women, probably because the strong women didn't allow them to have any control.

Lauren loved her family and was a strong woman as well. Jim knew they were and it was one of the reasons why he loved her so much because she was very opinionated and his wife would make sure that she said what she needed to say. Jim knew that about his wife, which caused lots of debates in their marriage because both of them thought things should be their way. His wife didn't mind submitting as long as you were not leading her in the wrong direction and that is why they made an awesome team together.

Lauren and Jim had everything packed and ready for the trip and had already let the boys know that they would be gone for a week. The boys had no plans of coming home until Thanksgiving break and Jim and Lauren both couldn't wait to see their young men. They were both so smart and pressing towards their goal in their careers. Both of them were in steady relationships with two women who were raised right by their parents and had good heads on their shoulders.

It was getting late in the day so they both decided that they would pick up some Japanese food from their favorite spot and maybe get caught up on some tv. They ordered, picked up the food and headed back home. Lauren split the meal between both, got some drinks and headed to their den area in their master suite. They ate and watched some TV until the TV started to watch them back. They went to sleep and slept very peacefully until the next day.

When the couple woke up the sun was already shining on their faces. Lauren looked at the time and it was 7:00 a.m. She thought that she would get up and get a head start in the bathroom. She brushed her teeth and prepared to get in the shower.

She was taking off her clothes when she heard Jim moving around in the bedroom. She knew that it wouldn't be long before he would need to use the bathroom, so she hurried her shower along so that she wouldn't be in his way.

Lauren wanted to finish up so they had time to talk about the plan of what time they wanted to be on the road. They agreed that the next hour would be good so that they could stop by and get breakfast while on the road.

Check in time wasn't until 3 p.m., but they decided when getting to Wilmington they would do some looking around, shop at the grocery store and get some dinner before going to the room so that on the first day they could just relax and enjoy the scenery. Lauren loved the plan and said that she would love to buy herself another bathing suit because the hotel had an indoor swimming pool and jacuzzi. Jim said that could happen, so they continued to get their stuff in order to be able to leave in the next hour. The hour went by super-fast and both of them were done with loading the car to go on their much-needed quality time vacation.

Lauren and Jim did a lot of talking and planning when they were on trips and Lauren was able to do a lot of writing in a different setting which gave her plenty of ideas. They stopped to get some breakfast and got right back on the road. Lauren didn't do a lot of driving; however she loved that her husband Jim loved to drive. She just sat back, relaxed and listened to the jazz music to relax her mind.

The resort was about three hours away, which was the perfect travel time to them because it was just enough time to enjoy the ride but not enough time to get too tired and have to take a break. Jim loved to drive his wife around while she relaxed because he knew that made her happy. He knew when his wife was happy, life was good.

About two hours into the ride, they stopped at a store to fill up the gas and Lauren woke up and said that she would go in and get some snacks for the rest of the trip. Lauren found out what Jim wanted and went in to get it. She decided that she should go to the bathroom so that she wouldn't have to go later. Lauren finished in the store and walked back to the car to her husband. Jim was already back in the car listening to his jazz music and watching his wife come back to the car. They got back on the road and enjoyed their snacks.

About an hour later, they were already enjoying the view of Wilmington Beach. The weather was perfect. They loved to go to the beach when it wasn't scorching hot and thought it was best to go around October or the beginning of November. The resort was beautiful and there were people just walking on the strip enjoying the water, shopping and food.

They pulled up to a grocery store and decided since they were already at their destination, they could pick up the groceries they needed for the room. They picked up breakfast foods, snacks for leisure time, some sandwich items and ingredients to make a small baked spaghetti. Lauren always thought that having food in the condo was always a good idea just in case they didn't want to leave. They would have what they needed to be comfortable.

Lauren and Jim checked into the resort and unloaded the car to bring in everything that they would need. They decided that they would walk the strip to do a little personal shopping. They had seen a couple of good steak restaurants that they could order dinner in and be comfortable for that night.

Lauren and Jim enjoyed hanging out on the strip and thought it would be best to go in and maybe watch some TV. The condo was very nice. It had two bedrooms, a full kitchen loaded with everything you needed to prepare dinner, and it had a jacuzzi inside the master bedroom. Lauren loved a jacuzzi and her husband knew that when traveling this had to be a must have for their room. Lauren had never had one in the actual room but now this model was a must have for her. There was everything you needed in the room calling for a good week of relaxation.

Lauren was really looking to spend some quality time with her husband away from the house and possibly bring a little romance back into their relationship. Lauren realized being a wife and doing the everyday hustle and bustle of life caused them to miss out on much needed time to keep the relationship interesting. Lauren knew how much her husband loved seeing her in her Victoria lingerie, so she had decided to give him a show. Lauren decided that after they finished unpacking the bags that she would get the dinner ready to be served and maybe watch a movie.

Lauren and Jim were sitting down enjoying dinner and relaxing and decided to keep on relaxing by enjoying the jacuzzi that was located in their master suite. She got everything prepared to get into the jacuzzi and laid out some of the surprises that she had for her husband. She and Jim got into the tub; and the water was perfect. Lauren had put bubbles and Epsom salt into the tub so that their muscles could also be relaxed.

After about 20 minutes of relaxing in the

environment the mood began to shift, and it was now time to enjoy some much-needed alone time. Jim took the lead, and Lauren was enjoying the romance building.

Jim took Lauren to the bed and was on the top when Lauren noticed that something wasn't looking right in Jim's face. She noticed that he seemed to be frozen in one position and that his eyes were not focusing. Lauren called his name twice and Jim was moaning as if he was trying to say something and couldn't.

Lauren had a little medical background, so she was trying to put her finger on what was happening in her state of fear. She switched position to lay Jim on his back and to be able to call the ambulance. Jim was confused and his left side seemed to not be moving that well. When Lauren looked in his face, she could tell that his face was drooping on one side and that he was probably having a stroke!

Lauren was scared but she remained calm while she told the paramedics what she was seeing. The operator said that someone would be there soon and was asking questions to see if her husband was aware. Jim seemed to be panicking, and he was moving towards the end of the bed trying to understand why he was not able to move his left side. Lauren was trying to tell him that he would be okay but, before she could say anything, Jim was falling headfirst off the bed almost hitting his head on the end of the nightstand by the bed. Lauren kicked in overdrive and caught him by throwing her entire body in the way of the nightstand and his head so that he wouldn't hurt himself.

Before long Lauren was stuck with nothing on and her husband on top of her, who was much larger in weight on her lap, confused as he fell off of the bed. It seemed like an hour but there was a knock on the room door announcing to be the firemen.

Lauren tried to lay her husband safely on the floor so that she could use her strength to pull herself up to let them inside the door. She grabbed a pair of pants and a shirt and with the speed of lightning put the clothes on so that she wouldn't be naked in front of a room full of strangers. She was so embarrassed when four firemen walked in, and she felt that everyone was watching her. Everything felt like a bad dream and she couldn't wake up. She pinched herself, shook her head, blinked, but the nightmare was still there.

The men started asking her the same questions that she knew was protocol, so she gave them the answers that they wanted. The room door was already open and in came another man and a woman who were the paramedics. They confirmed that he was having a stroke and was already giving him some medicine that would slow any brain bleeding down so it wouldn't cause any more damage on top of what it had already caused.

One of the paramedics walked by the room and noticed the Epsom salt in a container and asked Lauren what it was. Lauren told the paramedic that it was Epsom salt for the bath. The paramedic asked if Jim was on any drugs that they needed to know about. Lauren was having mixed feelings about the line of questioning but snapped out of it to realize that this was also part of the procedure of helping her husband properly.

Lauren was grabbing her purse and was glad that at least the paramedics were able to get her husband covered up so that he could keep his dignity. Lauren was in shock. She started to panic because she wasn't too familiar with the area and knew that their much-needed vacation had turned into a complete nightmare! Tears started to run down her face and they wouldn't stop.

Her chest started to get very heavy when she realized that the elevator was too full and that she was going to have to either wait or take the stairs so that she wouldn't get left behind. She didn't know where the hospital was but she knew they said that it was a stroke trauma center and that he would be in good hands.

Lauren took the stairs and met them at the ambulance where the driver told her that timing was everything in these situations and that they would be riding very fast to the hospital with the sirens on. He asked if she had ever ridden in an ambulance and Lauren told him no. She was still waiting to wake up as she heard her husband mumbling, not speaking like she was used to him doing.

Lauren sat in front and thought that she would call and let someone know. She called her mother and told her mother, and her mother was very sad and said that she would come down if she needed her to.

Lauren's mother was a doctor and Jim was the son she had never had. Jim and her mother had a great relationship, and her mother was very sorry that she had to go through it. Her mother let her know that she shouldn't let the kids know right now because she didn't want them to panic. Her mother told Lauren that she would let Jim's sister and brothers know because that was all the family that he had left living.

Lauren cried all the way to the hospital because she realized that she was going to need to be strong for her husband. The ride seemed to be about twenty minutes, which gave her enough time to calm down a little. She had so many emotions and didn't know how to deal with them at all. She was scared, embarrassed and mad at the same time. A part of her was upset with her husband because he wouldn't listen to her about going to see a doctor. The embarrassment came because she thought of the activity that was happening during the stroke, and she was scared of what his condition would be after the stroke. She had a fear of the unknown and her husband was always the one who helped her deal with these situations and now who would help her?

Lauren was snapped out of her thoughts when she realized that the ambulance was coming to a stop at a big emergency hospital. They were getting out with her husband and coming to help her out as well. There was no need to stop by the waiting room. Everyone went straight into the back.

Phone calls must have happened because when the paramedics brought her husband in, a doctor met them at the door and they took Jim in for a CT scan and other tests and took Lauren into an emergency room where there was a computer and a doctor on the phone. Lauren noticed that the doctor seemed to be working from home and realized with telemedicine and computers anything was possible.

They immediately started asking her questions about her husband's medical history, which Lauren let them know that her husband was healthy and didn't have any signs. She mentioned that he had said something about a headache about two weeks ago and that her husband was so tough that he said that he would be okay and didn't need to check on it. They asked questions about his primary care doctor and Lauren told the doctor that he doesn't see one unless there is an issue and that he was a healthy man. They asked if he ever suffered from high blood pressure and again Lauren told them that they mentioned him having high blood pressure when he left the military, but he never followed up on it.

Lauren told the doctor that he hadn't had any of the signs of a stroke and that he didn't smoke, drink or use any street drugs. When she asked about numbness or weakness on one side, headaches or dizziness she told the doctor no but thought about her having some of those same symptoms about three months ago.

Lauren felt defeated and just wanted her husband to be okay. She thought about the children and how his sister would feel knowing that her brother had a stroke and that she was already caring for their cousin who had had four strokes. Lauren started crying again and this time a panic attack came with it. The doctor called a nurse in the room to ensure that she was okay and asked if she needed to be seen as well. Lauren said that she was okay and when could she see her husband?

The doctor seemed to be busy reading something else on the screen, so she didn't answer her question.

A nurse came into the room while the doctor was on the monitor to confirm the results that Jim had a major stroke caused by high blood pressure which caused a brain bleed on his right side. The doctor said that right now he was paralyzed completely on his left side which could also control his speech and other things in his brain not to function properly. She said that this could or could not be permanent depending on how fast the bleeding dries up so that he could get use of his limbs again.

Lauren barely heard anything after the fact that her husband's condition may be permanent. She didn't have time to process it long before they were bringing her husband back in the room to put him on monitors so that they could monitor every moment of his life. Lauren noticed that they had put him a hospital gown on but it was wet in his private area which meant that he couldn't control his bladder as well.

Lauren grabbed his hand, and her husband still was unable to say words that she understood. He was alert and speaking a language that only she could understand letting her know that he was sorry and that he loved her. Lauren had to step out while more doctors were coming in to help him and the ICU room was very crowded.

Lauren thought this would be a good time to update her mother when she received a phone call from Jim's sister Jamie. Jamie was crying and asking if he was okay and that she was coming down. Lauren told Jamie to make sure that her husband Chris did the driving because she wanted them to be safe in their travel. Lauren gave her the hospital they were at, and she had to get back inside with her brother.

Lauren loved Jim's sister Jamie and her husband Chris because they were a great tagged team much like her and Jim and they could always depend on them no matter what it was. Lauren told them about the car and all of their belongings were at the resort and that she didn't know what they would do. Chris and Jamie said that they would take care of it and to let them know where they were staying. Lauren gave them all the details, and they said that they would be at the hospital in about 1 hour and 45 minutes. Lauren felt better knowing that she would have family close in the area because she didn't have any family in Wilmington.

When she got back in the room Jim was trying to talk and tell her that he had to go to the bathroom, but it was too late he was already going. Jim's blood pressure read 198/116 and his pulse rate was also very high. The doctors let her know that he was on a medicine that would help regulate his blood pressure because right now the blood pressure was the main concern, and they didn't want another stroke. Lauren knew that once people have a stroke then they were at a higher risk of having another one.

Lauren grabbed her husband's hand and prayed that God would get them through this struggle and that he would keep her strong to deal with the challenges that would come afterwards. Lauren knew this would be a long ride for Jamie and she had to ensure that she stayed strong in her Faith so that she could endure.

Jim and Lauren were in the room and the ICU nurse had left the room. Jim started looking very weak and seemed to fall off to sleep. Lauren looked at him and the monitor and noticed that his blood pressure had dropped completely low and Jim was losing consciousness. Lauren went outside yelling for the nurse to come back to the room and they had to take him off the medicine that they were using to regulate his blood pressure because it was dropping too fast and too low.

Jim started to get his energy back up, but Lauren had to get her own heart rate to slow down. She was so close to becoming a widow, but God had another plan. Lauren decided that she was not going anywhere because she had to make sure that the doctors and nurses were going to do their job in helping to keep her husband alive.

Jim's blood pressure started to go back up to what was normal in this condition and Jim seemed to want to get some much-needed rest. Lauren went outside to get a little fresh air after kissing her husband and letting him know that she wouldn't be far away.

She was walking out the door when she saw Jamie coming down the hall towards her brother's room. She hugged Lauren and both of them cried knowing that the situation was hard but different for each one of them. Lauren filled Jamie in on what had just happened, and that Jim was stable and getting some rest. Lauren told Jamie that she was glad that she had made it safely and that she was glad that Jim wouldn't be left alone without family.

Lauren went out to fill her mother and family in on everything and her mother was there to help her keep it all together. Her mother said that it would be a good idea to let the young men find out in person. Lauren knew that her boys were very mature and calm so she said that she would have them to go to her mother's house so that she would let them know because Lauren knew that she wouldn't be able to leave right now and when she mentioned being transferred to a hospital closer to home so that they could be around family the medical professionals said that he was not stable enough to be moved but that it could be arranged maybe later. Lauren just wanted her husband to get back to normal, whatever that may look like.

Lauren finished up with talking to her mother and thought it would be best to go to the chapel to get some much-needed time with God. She sat down, prayed and cried out to God about her situation. Lauren had so many emotions in one. She was scared, sad, mad and confused. She thought about what the doctors said about his condition being permanent. She thought about how before that her husband was so independent and didn't want to have help from anyone and how he could now need help which would also play on his mind as well. She cried because the boys may not be able to see their father in this condition because they were used to their father being strong. She was crying and praying so much that she didn't notice that the chaplain had come in and sat down to make sure that she didn't need to talk about it.

The chaplain was a male who seemed very concerned about her health. Lauren let him know that she would be fine, but she was letting God know her fears and that she was going to get into the word of God to gain some clarity. The chaplain gave her a card and told her to use it anytime she needed to and that, if he needed to come into the room for prayer, just call him. Lauren said that she would use it if she needed it, but she just needed some alone time with the Lord right now.

Lauren was glad that Jamie and her husband Chris were there because she was going to have to figure out what she was going to do with the rest of this trip. She was in deep thought when her phone rang, and it was Jamie and Chris letting her know that they were getting something to eat and did she want anything.

Lauren realized that she hadn't had anything to eat since the incident, and she didn't even realize it. Jamie said that she would pick her up something anyway and that Jim was asking about her so she should head back to the room. Jamie and her husband Chris were the best family anyone could ask for. Jamie had already got her brother's keys and the condo key, and they were going to take care of everything.

Lauren thanked God because she didn't know what she would do. It worked out well because Jamie and Chris would have somewhere to stay while they were here and they would make sure all their things were packed in their car. Lauren knew that she would stay with her husband and that she would probably never see that resort room again.

Lauren was walking back to the ICU room where her husband was when she noticed that her husband was trying to talk to the nurse. Her husband noticed her, and he smiled with his eyes as if she was the answer that he needed. When she walked into the room her husband was able to talk with her. Lauren was very excited but also noticed that he didn't sound like his normal self. The words were slurring together and she still noticed that when he smiled only the right side of his face would move. She figured that all of this was related to muscles not responding but this was at least an improvement from earlier.

Lauren held his hand and told him that it will be okay and that nothing was impossible with God. Her husband smiled again and held her hand. The nurse told Lauren that her husband would have to do speech, occupational and physical therapy in a rehab hospital so that they could continue to monitor his vitals. Lauren asked if they could possibly find one that was closer to their home and the nurse said that she would get a social worker to come into the room to discuss it further. Lauren thanked the nurse, and the nurse went out of the room so that she could spend some quality time with her husband.

Jim had a lot to say, and Lauren listened best as she could. Lauren let Jim know that his sister Jamie and her husband Chris had already taken care of the room and were going to stay there so that they wouldn't lose any money. Lauren asked Jim if he had to use the bathroom because she noticed that he was a little wet in that area. Jim said he didn't, and Lauren grabbed the urinal and said that he could try. Lauren held the urinal and grabbed some gloves from the wall and helped her husband use the bathroom. The sadness came back to her mind when she realized that this would probably be what she had to do until he got back to himself, and she had to hold back tears so that she wouldn't discourage her husband in any kind of way of getting better.

He finished and Lauren ensured that she wiped him and put the urine to the side so that the nurses could chart it for their records. Lauren threw the gloves away and washed her hands. Jim didn't have any movement on his left side, but his right side had all his normal strength. Lauren thanked God that it wasn't the worst and that she was thankful that it didn't go another way.

A doctor came in while she was in deep thoughts and introduced himself as the chief doctor on the neuro team and he came to check on him and answer any questions. The doctor told her again that it was caused by high blood pressure and may have been prevented with medications if Jim was seeing a regular primary care doctor. Lauren was feeling a little upset, but Jim was also listening.

The doctor performed some tests to see how his mind was reacting after the stroke. Jim was able to pass the test with flying colors which made Lauren very happy to see that the stroke didn't affect his mental abilities. The doctor told them that they would be in the

ICU until they got the blood pressure under control and then they would use medications to keep it under control. The doctor mentioned that it would be possible to move him to an in-care rehab hospital for his therapy closer to their home once everything gets stabilized.

Lauren listened and took notes of all the doctors and the information they had given her. It was getting later in the evening and Lauren thought it would be best to get something to eat. The hospital put Jim on a strict diet, but she ensured that he ate at least a little of his food so that he could keep his strength up. She let him know that she was going to pick up something from the cafeteria and Jim shook his head that he would be fine until she came back.

As she was walking to the cafeteria her oldest son Jeremiah was calling her on the phone. She picked it up and he was already at his grandmother's house and heard the news. Lauren asked if he was okay. He then asked if his father was okay? Lauren told him that he was stable, however his speech wasn't all that good right now. She let him know that his father was a fighter and everything was going to be okay.

Her son wanted to drive to Wilmington, but Lauren told him not to come yet because they were working on getting him transferred to a rehab facility. Jeremiah seemed to have taken the news well and so Lauren told him to make sure his brother got to his grandma's house safely and to call her when he did. Jeremiah was very mature and acted much like his father so she knew that he would watch over his brother. Her youngest son Joseph was also very responsible, and Lauren was glad that her husband had been there to help her raise such honorable young men.

When Lauren got into the cafeteria she decided on a ham and cheese sandwich, some chips and a cookie for later. She grabbed her soda and was on her way back to her husband's room. When she got in, she noticed that her husband had already fallen to sleep. She got in the chair and was very quiet so that he could rest. She covered him up with another blanket and grabbed her a blanket as well. She had already figured that she wouldn't sleep too well tonight because the only thing that was in the room was a recliner chair. She let it back, covered up and ate a little bit of her dinner.

Before long she had fallen asleep with her hand inside her husband's hand. Lauren was asleep for about two hours when she was awakened by a nurse getting blood from her husband. Lauren didn't know why they had to get so much blood so often, but it seemed every two hours someone else needed blood. She didn't realize that the hospital was filled with a bunch of vampires until she had to stay overnight with her husband.

After about three more interruptions from nurses or doctors Lauren was awakened by daylight outside. She and Jim had made it overnight and she had a major crook in her neck. Jim woke up staring at her with a smile and seemed to be content that she was there with him. Lauren looked over at the monitor with the vitals and noticed that the top number on his blood pressure was looking in normal range, but the bottom number was still over 100. Lauren knew that it would be a process, and she knew that the doctors were doing all they could do to help her husband get better.

Lauren noticed that her husband was only on clear liquids and the nurse said that he had to pass a swallowing test before eating solid foods. Another team of healthcare providers came in and they were the PT/OT and speech therapist. They explained that they would be coming in to help her husband with physical strength, doing his everyday duties and learning how to wake the muscles up so that he could speak better.

Lauren understood that all these care providers were very important so that her husband could start working his body to get back to his regular self. They let her know that they would be in twice a week so that they could see what he could do on his own.

Jim looked very excited about working out because he loved to stay in shape. Even in his current condition she knew he wanted to get out of bed and start working out but she knew all of it would be a process. They left her a schedule of when they would be coming and said that she could also be in the room so that she can learn what she can help him work on as well when they were able to go home.

Lauren agreed and said that she would see them soon. Whatever she had to do to get her husband back to his strong sexy self she was willing to do but she still had so many questions that she wanted to ask and didn't know why she was still feeling hurt, alone and confused. One thing that she knew for sure was that God didn't make any mistakes and that he had his hands on the whole situation.

Lauren was sleeping well when she heard her husband call her name and say that he had to use the bathroom. She jumped up, grabbed some gloves and the urinal to do the regular ritual when she realized that he was doing more than the regular ritual. She buzzed the nurse to help bring her what she needed and looked at her husband to see that he looked very embarrassed. Lauren assured him that it would be okay and that she would make sure that he got cleaned up.

The nurse came in and helped slide a bedpan under his bottom and then put the blanket back over him for some privacy. She said that she would step out and to call her when he was done. Lauren kissed her husband and held his hand to let him know that it would all be okay. She could see her husband holding back tears showing his emotions of not being comfortable with his condition. Lauren held her tears back for his strength and after about five minutes he was finished. She paged the nurse, and the nurse came in with wipes and a new gown just in case it was needed. Lauren helped clean her husband up well and made sure that his clothes and bed sheets were also cleaned.

Jim seemed to be satisfied with how helpful his wife was in helping him with his personal care. Lauren took the gloves off, washed her hands and covered her husband up while lying on the corner of the bed right beside him. She didn't know how long they were going to be in the ICU, but it felt so good just to lay in the bed next to the man she married. Jim tried to make his left side hold her, but nothing was happening which seemed to upset him. Lauren understood the frustration so she got up to lie on the other side of him so that he could hold her. It wasn't much longer before both of them fell asleep as best they could.

Lauren was awakened two hours later by the nurse who came in to get blood for the lab. Jim was still sleeping so Lauren got back in the chair to give the nurses access to Jim's arm and the monitors.

Lauren realized that she needed a good night's sleep somewhere in a bed, but she didn't want to leave without her husband. She thought about the wedding vows and realized that they were really living out their vows, especially on the part that said for good or bad and through sickness and health.

She thought about her life before marrying Jim and all the time she told him to go to the doctor, and he wouldn't go. Anger began to rise in her but she then thought about how God had blessed her with a great man who gave her all that she could ask for and realized that if she had to do it all over again, she would even if that meant reliving the scariest thing that she ever had to deal with. She gave God his praise and prayed for her entire family. God gave her peace, and she went back to sleep and slept for another three hours.

Lauren woke up to her sister-in-law Jamie and her husband Chris talking to Jim. She got herself together and talked to Jamie about her car and some clothes. Chris let her know that they had everything packed and her car was already outside. Jamie said that the condo slept nicely and thanked them for letting them stay in it so they wouldn't have to pay for a hotel room. Lauren let Jamie and Chris know that they could stay at the resort for a week and if they needed to stay longer they would extend the stay.

Lauren knew that was the least that she could do because Jamie and Chris always came through with whatever they needed to do to help anyone. Jamie and Chris let them know that they would be at the hospital most of the day so it would be a good time for her to take some time for herself. Lauren figured getting a hotel room close by the hospital probably would be best so that she could be in close proximity but was interrupted on her thoughts by a room full of doctors.

There was a team of doctors making their rounds checking on Jim and saying that he would be moved out of ICU to a stroke recovering unit so that he could start therapy. That was great news for everyone and that would give more room for Lauren to work with. In about three hours they were moving Jim to a new unit which had a shower in the room, which was more great news.

While they transferred Jim, Chris stayed with him and Jamie and Lauren went to the car so that she could get some clothes. Lauren and Jamie vented a little to each other and offered each other support.

While walking back to the room, Lauren got a call from her youngest son who seemed to be taking it hard that his father wasn't at his best. Lauren let him know that they were moving his father from the ICU and that he would be starting therapy, which was going to be important to getting his father back on track.

Joseph let his mother know that he didn't want to see his father at his worst and that he would wait a little before coming down.

Lauren said that would be a good idea because the plan was to get him transferred closer to home for his therapy. Lauren let her son know that everything would be okay and that she loved him. Jamie grabbed Lauren's hand to help her with her emotions, and they walked back towards the hospital.

Lauren and Jamie walked into the new room and noticed that it was a larger room. They had a recliner and another long chair that could be used as a bed. The bathroom was big, and it had a full shower. Lauren was a little more excited and thought that she could be a little more comfortable. She had also put some of Jim's comfortable jogging pants in her bag so that he would have something comfortable to wear when he did therapy.

She was putting her bag away when the therapy team and speech therapist came into the room. They were there to perform the swallow test to see if he would be able to eat real food. After doing a couple of tests they decided that Jim would be able to have a regular diet. Jim seemed excited about that and even said some words. Lauren smiled and kissed her husband on his lips and Jim gave her a half smile.

The other therapist was able to see what kind of strength Jim had on his own and they realized that his left side was totally asleep, however he was able to hold himself up with the strength of his other side. Jim loved to be pushed and did all the hard exercises as well which made Lauren very happy. The therapist was teaching him how to walk all over again and do his regular daily activities in moderations. Lauren was very emotional seeing that her husband, who didn't like any help now depended on help with doing simple day-to-day activities and at that moment he would need lots of help at home.

Three Months Later...

A lot had changed in three months. With medicines daily Jim's blood pressure was under control. His left side still had not awakened up fully, however Jim had learned to do a lot on his own utilizing the strength of his right side.

The boys were able to come to the rehab and learn how to care for their father so that the whole household could ensure his safety. Jamie and her husband Chris were very helpful and helped set things up at home for Jim's arrival. Things like a chairlift, a bathroom remodel, a ramp for the front of the house and safety bars had to be utilized so that Jim would be able to manage in his own house.

With help Jim was able to do a lot of things on his own, but assistance needed to be in place just in case he fell and needed help. Jim had to always have someone home with him and there were schedules put in place so that he wouldn't be alone. Jim couldn't drive and he had to do rehab at home twice a week so that he could continue to get stronger every day. The doctor told him that it could be a couple of years before his left side wakes completely up, but the brain bleed was getting smaller which was great news! Jim was able to talk like his normal self so that was already an improvement. The speech therapist released him and said it wasn't needed and that he could put that time in getting more physical therapy and occupational therapy so he could get stronger in those areas.

Jim and Lauren were able to talk about some of the things, but Jim was now a regular patient at the doctor. He had to see all kinds of specialists so that they could ensure that he didn't have a repeat. The medicines changed here and there until they found something that worked right. The side effects to the blood pressure pills created other issues which caused Jim not to be able to perform like he used to, however Lauren loved him anyway and said that God would fully heal him when the time was right. This caused Jim to get a little depressed, but Lauren constantly stroked his ego and told him that he would be all she ever needed and that she didn't want to go anywhere. This helped Jim push more with his therapy and day by day he got a little stronger.

Even though their marriage had changed drastically it only brought them together more spiritually. Jim was in a wheelchair most of the time, but Lauren would always help him with everything from therapy and, with helping, pushed the military man to his max. They were a great team, and everyone saw how much they genuinely loved one another. Even though sometimes they would get dirty looks because she was parking in the handicap spots and seemed to not need it she didn't care because she would do whatever she needed to do to support her husband.

Lauren needed a stress reliever, so she decided to start doing Zumba at the MEC with Dwaine on Mondays and Wednesdays. She decided to take her husband with her so that he could get extra workouts. Both of them were very hesitant at first but when she arrived and noticed that the members were so nice and helped her get the wheelchair and her husband in, she loved it. Not only did the coach and members embrace her, but they also encouraged her husband too. Jim enjoyed it because it was not just for women, but he was able to work his muscles which taught him how to train his mind to do what he needed it to do.

This Zumba family was the best they ever had. They were the very first married couple, but then because of how hard her husband worked in the wheelchair, it started to inspire other couples to come and even other people with disabilities. This Zumba class was a place that was built on Faith, Fitness, Family and Fun and it was indeed the place to be.

Jim was so determined to get back to his normal self that he would push himself so hard that Lauren would tell him that he had to get some rest. He didn't let the stroke stop him. He continued to be involved in teaching in church and working out to get stronger by the day.

Before long Jim was making great progress. He knew how to do his own showers, and take care of his own hygiene, even cook with one arm and get out of the wheelchair and walk with a cane. He was making a lot of progress because he was determined to do better.

Lauren decided to get her Healthcare Management

Bachelor's degree while she was at home with Jim so that she could keep herself busy. She did online classes and took care of her husband day to day. Money wasn't an issue because her husband was able to get his military benefits and disability, and Lauren was able to get money for being her husband's caregiver. Life wasn't normal but it was their new normal. Everyone jumped in to help and the boys graduated from college and got jobs close so that they could help support their father.

Two Years Later...

Jim and Lauren were packing for their first trip since the stroke happened. Both had some heartburn but told themselves that they wouldn't let a stroke stop them from traveling and living out their dreams. They were going to stay in a mountain cabin in Gatlinburg, Tennessee. It was Lauren's birthday month, which was in December, and they were overdue for some quality time. They were going to stay a week in the mountains and needed to just get away. Lauren realized that she was suffering with some PTSD when it came to an intimate time with her husband, but she was determined to work through these differences and get their relationship back to normal.

Even though therapy was a new part of their weekly routine, and a wheelchair, walker and lots of doctor's appointments Lauren and Jim made a new normal life. They kept God first and learned that even great marriages will have struggles. However, as long as both of you keep the vows that you said in front of your

Heavenly Father and the witnesses you must adjust to whatever struggles you are given so that your marriage will always be protected. Lauren and Jim realized that through the struggles was where they were able to show God more in their marriage which caused others to look up to their relationship and really learn the meaning of what true love really was and how to help other marriages get through some of their tough times with health struggles.

Jim was now an advocate for black men's health and teaching them the importance of going to the doctor regularly because when they don't take care of themselves, they harm others around them as well. Jim offered information on different screenings and how to recognize the signs of a stroke. He was such a great advocate.

Lauren and the boys learned how to be caregivers and did it with love. Lauren and Jim went to marriage counseling together to help with their most intimate moments and to help one another deal with the trauma behind the struggle that they both had to live through. The boys were still doing well in their careers, and both were engaged to be married. Jim and Lauren were a couple everyone honored and respected because they truly knew what it meant to really keep the vows that they both said in front of God and the witnesses.

THE END

FINANCIAL AND INFIDELITY STRUGGLES

Melissa was sitting at her job thinking about whether she should get a second job. Melissa was not a mother yet but a wife to Jeff who was a mother's boy who couldn't keep a job if you held it for him. He always would land pretty good jobs but always found an excuse for why he couldn't get back to the job.

Melissa was a Bank Manager at Corporate Bank which was a well-known bank on the East coast and West Coast. She had been there for 12 years and had experience in every role in retail and was very good at her job. She had built an excellent rapport with her customers and her employees and had received so many awards that she was running out of places to hang them.

She and Jeff had only been married for three years, and she thought it would get better, but it seemed to be getting worse. Jeff had a job with Food Lion in the produce department where he was guaranteed his hours and made decent money with benefits. Both worked daytime hours, which put them in a good position to spend time with each other at night.

Melissa was the breadwinner and the one that had to come home to take care of what Jeff didn't do. Melissa and Jeff lived in a three-bedroom home in a good neighborhood. Jeff and Melissa overall had an okay relationship when his mother stayed out of it but struggled with finances because Jeff didn't know how to budget at all. He loved to spend money on things that he didn't need like game systems and new clothes and cars, so he could brag to his friends that he had it going on.

Melissa didn't really care for his friends because they only wanted to chase fake dreams, eat, mess up and play video games all day. They always wanted to come to their house because they still lived with their mothers and didn't have a place of their own.

Melissa and Jeff were in their thirties and Melissa was very career driven but Jeff couldn't get a steady career. Melissa loved her husband despite the circumstances and knew that it wasn't anything that the Lord couldn't work out for her. She attended church regularly and was very involved in serving. Melissa knew that paying her tithes faithfully was the right thing to do so she always paid them off the top of every check she got. Jeff, on the other hand, wouldn't do right with how he spent his money, and this was one of the biggest struggles they had in their marriage. They had all their finances joint at first until Jeff took money for bills and brought a new game system and didn't pay one of the main bills. Melissa became very upset and decided that she would also have a separate account for her direct deposit so that she could make sure all the bills got paid.

Melissa struggled with doing things separately because she knew that this wasn't right because it was causing separation in their marriage. She had suggested therapy for their marriage, but Jeff declined and said that he didn't need anyone to tell him how to be in his marriage and manage his finances. She felt that it was needed but arguing with him wasn't what she wanted to do.

Melissa was finishing up her day managing her location when she realized that her next career path in the bank was a District Manager and she didn't want to be one, so she started realizing that she wanted to go back to school to get her psychology degree. She had a bachelor's degree in business and administration, but she had always wanted to be a therapist.

Every time she thought about it she realized that her husband was too unstable and that she wouldn't have the support she needed to focus on school, work and being a wife. She also knew that she was thirty-two and wasn't getting any younger and if she ever wanted to be a mother she might need to start now.

Her husband Jeff wanted children but Melissa didn't want to complicate their marriage anymore because she felt that having a child would be more on her because her husband wasn't helping too much with finances and at home. She could see herself being a mother, but she just felt that the time just wasn't right. Melissa was strong in her faith and knew that God's time was not her time and it would happen when it needed to happen.

Jeff's mother was pressuring her about having a grandchild and even made comments that insinuated that she wasn't good enough for her son. Jeff's mother didn't have but one son and she didn't want to let him live his own life. Jeff's mother would still give him money to buy the things he wanted, which wasn't helping Melissa teach her husband how to be responsible. He would quit a job before finding another and move really slow to find another because his mother would give him everything that he needed. Melissa realized that she may have married her husband too fast because she was getting older and felt it was important to start a family before she got too old.

Jeff and Melissa met in the church, and both were trying to wait until they were married to have sex. Melissa had never been with a man sexually. On the other hand, Jeff was with one partner before her, and they were in a long relationship that ended up not working because she wanted to see other people. They dated for about eight months before Jeff asked to marry her, and she didn't decline because he was handsome, smart and serving in the same church that she was in. His mother seemed to like her so she thought that everything would work out well.

They had a small wedding with family on the beach and everything was great. Melissa realized that Jeff was her first but he was very good at doing what he did so she may have looked over some of the other qualities that he didn't have. It was ok for the first year, but things didn't change in year number two. Now they were three years in, and Jeff was still in and out of jobs and talking to his mother about everything that went on in their relationship.

She realized that being a mother's boy wasn't as bad as them not being on the same page with their finances. Melissa had always been a good money manager, however Jeff loved to spend money on material things. Jeff loved to look like he had it all together on the outside while struggling to get it together on the inside. It was starting to be a real challenge because Melissa loved to do right by God. She was an advocate for the book of Malachi and how paying your tithes and offering would always work for her.

She knew that if she didn't pay her tithes they may have gone under a long time ago when Jeff used the mortgage money to buy some personal items of his own and loan the rest to a friend who was not going to pay the money back. Melissa had to do something that she didn't want to do like going into her retirement funds to make ends meet and Jeff seemed like he didn't make a bad choice with helping a friend. Melissa was fasting and praying, and she knew that honoring her marriage was right by the Lord, but on the other hand, she was looking for signs that God wanted her to go another way.

She was tired of always being the talk of his family while she was the one carrying the household because he couldn't keep a job. She had encouraged counseling, and her husband was never on board. Something was going to have to change because this marriage was starting to look like a dead end.

Melissa woke up and noticed that Jeff was still asleep and should have been to work an hour ago. Melissa yelled Jeff's name and told him to get up to get ready for work. Jeff covered back up and said that he was tired because he and his friends stayed up last night to play the new Call of Duty game and didn't get into bed until two hours ago.

Melissa was very angry. She had so many things that she knew she was supposed to do as a wife but waking her husband up for a job wasn't one of them. Melissa snatched that cover off him and told him that if he gets written up again for his attendance he could get fired and if he got fired, he would deal with the wrath!

Melissa went into the bathroom so that she could get herself together because she had a very important meeting with a potential business partner and she and her banker were going to be bringing his business from another bank which would really help their branch with their business.

Melissa picked out a nice black skirt suit and a white blouse. She loved shoes and pocketbooks and so she decided on her black and white striped heels and the pocketbook to match. She set off her outfit with the earrings to match her shoes and sprayed herself with some perfume. She had to say that she looked very business professional and was dressed to impress.

When she grabbed her keys to go out the door, she noticed that her husband was still in the bed. She decided to deal with that situation later because she couldn't let that cause her day to go bad because she needed to be on her A game for work today.

Melissa pulled into the parking lot at about 8 a.m. and waited for someone else to arrive to participate in the opening procedures. After the process

121

she went to her office to get herself prepared for her morning huddle and to meet with her banker so that they could pre-plan the business appointment. After that was completed, it was showtime and the doors opened at 8:55 a.m.

Melissa took her spot in the lobby to speak to the customers and that is when their appointment walked in. Melissa heard a lot about him from the city but had never met him in person. His name was Jeremiah Lyles, CEO of Capital Enterprises, which was a major marketing firm who owned a lot of other businesses. He was tall, dark, handsome and rich. He was a young bachelor who had never been married but had a long list of women who were trying to be his potential wife. He came from parents who were very successful, and they were very well off. He was opening a new business and wanted to open a new business account with all the benefits for merchants and payroll and getting a business line of credit to build his business credit for emergency purposes.

Melissa extended her hand to make him feel welcome and directed him into her banker's office. She offered him water, and he seemed very surprised and interested in her professionalism. He mentioned how professional she was and that if it was okay he wanted her to join them in the meeting. She assured him that she would be in the meeting and that she was taking some notes to ensure that the right products and services would be offered. He was very pleased.

The meeting went really well and Melissa was very good at her job and had trained her banker to be the same. They were able to gain his business and Mr. Lyles seemed very pleased with the service. The banker let him know that she would be following up with him in the morning and that another appointment was already set for two weeks to see how things were going.

Jeremiah gave both ladies his business cards and Melissa and the banker did the same. Jeremiah left the bank but not before telling Melissa it was very nice to meet her and that he couldn't wait to talk with her again. Melissa told him that her banker would definitely be calling him, and she hoped that the rest of his day was productive.

Melissa went to her office to check her messages and noticed that she had a message from her husband. She dialed his number to make sure that it was not urgent. Jeff answered the phone, and Melissa could hear him and his friends in the background doing what they knew how to do, which made her realize that he didn't go to work. Melissa tried not to get upset with him since she was at work, but she was boiling on the inside. Melissa told him that she was making sure that it wasn't urgent and that she would deal with him when she got home.

She hung up the phone and went back to work. She was walking out the office when she noticed that she had forgotten to put her wedding ring back on her finger. She took it off the night before to clean it and left it in the cleaner's because she was rushing when she noticed that her husband had overslept for work. She now realized that she may have given the wrong signal to Mr. Lyles, and she was embarrassed. Melissa thought it would be best not to bring up anything unless need be so she went out to manage her lobby.

Closing time was coming very fast so Melissa started to get an early start on the closing duties so that they could get out at a decent time. She was about to leave her office when the phone rang. She answered and it was Jeremiah. Melissa felt very nervous because she didn't know why he was calling.

When she answered, he made sure it was her and told her that he would like her to have lunch with him so that she could give him her opinion on the building he wanted to purchase. Melissa realized that she should at least tell him so that she could feel better about the business lunch. Melissa let Jeremiah know that she was married and that she didn't want to send any mixed messages and that she was embarrassed because she was rushing and left her ring in the cleaning solution.

Jeremiah laughed and said that he knew that someone as fine as she would already be taken and that if she wasn't he was going to try. Melissa told him that she was flattered, and she was sure that he would find the right one very soon. He invited her to a nice steak house close to her work which she knew to be very expensive and said that he would see her at noon. Melissa said that she would be there and would make sure she blocked her time so that she wouldn't get double booked. Jeremiah said that he was looking forward to seeing her tomorrow and they hung up.

Melissa felt better but was still a little nervous to know that Jeremiah was interested in her. Out of all the women he could have, he was interested in her. Melissa went to do her closing duties so that she could get out of the branch at least by 5:30.

Melissa and her banker made sure the branch was secured, set the alarms and went their separate ways. Melissa was driving home when her husband called and asked what she was going to cook and to make sure whatever it was to get enough for his friends. Melissa told him that she wasn't cooking for him or his friends and that those friends needed to be gone because she needed to have a conversation with him because the situation with him not working was getting out of control.

She hung up feeling very frustrated and asking God did she make the right decision or not? Melissa pulled up in the driveway to find Jeff's friends still at her house. She was very angry. She walked in the house, slammed the door and went straight to her bedroom.

She heard Jeff coming into the room and she was angry. He came in asking her to order pizza for him and his friends because he didn't have any more money. Melissa was boiling on the inside. She stormed out of the room and told his friends that playtime was over and that they needed to go home. Jeff seemed to be upset and told his friends that they didn't have to leave. Melissa hit the power on the game system and everyone got upset.

She said, "I will not repeat myself! I want everyone out now!!!"

Jeff was now looking confused and told his

friends that he would talk with them later. Melissa sat on the chair and asked Jeff again why he didn't go to work? Jeff said that he was tired. If looks could kill Jeff would have dropped dead. Melissa looked at Jeff and said the Bible speaks about when a man doesn't work, he doesn't eat. Melissa let him know that she was tired of him not working but spending up the money that she made on his friends and things that he didn't need. She told him that they were going to go to counseling or that she didn't want to do this anymore.

Jeff asked her if she was having that time of the month because she was extra moody. This made Melissa very upset. She got up and told him that he needed to sleep on the couch tonight and to not even think about getting in bed. Find yourself something to eat!

Melissa went into the room and slammed the door. Melissa thought that she would relax in the shower and listen to the word on audio. She knew that she might have been a little harsh, but she had been holding things in for a while now.

A couple of hours later, she thought that she would go fix her a sandwich and that is when she realized her husband's car was not there and he was gone. Melissa knew that he probably was either at his friend's house or went to his mother's house to talk about her. Either way she didn't care. Melissa got her clothes ready for tomorrow, ate her dinner and went to sleep early so that she could get plenty of rest.

Melissa woke up and noticed that she had slept all night long. She meant to call her husband to make sure they didn't go to bed mad at one another, but she fell asleep. She opened the door and noticed that her husband wasn't on the couch. She called his name and went into the spare bedrooms to not find him there either. She looked outside and noticed that his black F150 truck was not in the driveway. She got her phone and called him and there was no answer. She realized that it was after 7 a.m. and he would be at work right now.

She called the store only to find out that her husband wasn't there either. She called his mother, and his mother said that last night he hadn't come there either. She called one of his gaming friends that he was the closest to and he said that her husband was there but was coming out of the bathroom. She was waiting for him to come to the phone when she heard two female voices in the background. She was furious to know that there were women over there at this time meaning they must have stayed all night.

Jeff got on the phone very nonchalantly while talking with one of the females. Melissa was furious. She told Jeff to get his butt home right now or he would be staying there permanently. Jeff was trying to calm her down, explaining that it wasn't anything, but Melissa had already hung up the phone.

Melissa was praying and crying and hoping that this situation wasn't what it seemed to be. She then remembered that she asked God for a sign and hopefully this wasn't the sign that he was given her. She loved her husband and wanted it to work but there was no way that she would stay with him if he had violated their marriage vows.

About 20 minutes later Jeff came into the house trying to calm his wife down. She was so mad that she had to keep herself from throwing something at him. She asked God to help her, and asked Jeff why didn't he come home last night? Jeff tried to explain that since she was mad last night, he went out to get something to eat with his friend and ended up going back to his house. He then mentioned that his friend had invited two girls over to play the game with them, and they played all night, and everyone ended up falling asleep.

Melissa was looking at him strangely when she noticed a hickey on his neck. Melissa told Jeff to go look into the mirror and that she believed more than playing the game happened last night. Jeff knew he had to explain and realized that his wife knew that he was not telling the truth. Before he could do anything, else Melissa told him that she wanted him gone by the end of the week.

Jeff fell on his knees and said that he was stressed out because he lost his job, he had some drinks, and one thing led to the next and he had a one-night stand with one of the girls.

Melissa was very hurt. She felt that she had wasted her years, and she felt very stupid. She was willing to work with him being a mother's boy, and them having financial struggles but she was not going to be with a man who cheated on her.

Melissa told him that for now their relationship was over and that she didn't want to see him again. She told him not to call her and that she was going to work and he should be gone by the time she came home.

She went into her room to lock the door so that she could cry and get ready for work, but she felt defeated. She knew that she was fasting and praying looking for a sign and now that the sign was here, she wished that she had not asked for it.

Melissa heard Jeff at the door saying that he was going to his mother's house and that he loved her but would give her some time. Melissa told him that she loved him too and that she hoped that he would get the life God has for him. Melissa went into the bathroom and heard the front door close, meaning that Jeff was gone.

Melissa made a call to let her job know that she would be running a little late because a family emergency came up. She knew that she had some appointments today, so she decided that she needed to go into work in spite of the drama that she had just gone through.

Melissa put on a long black dress with a pink business coat with some colorful heels. She grabbed the purse that matched and went out the door looking good on the outside but feeling a mess on the inside. She got to work, and the bank was very busy, which kept her mind off of the drama she had at home.

Noon was approaching fast so she decided to leave a little early so that she could beat downtown traffic. She got to the restaurant about ten minutes early and Jeremiah was already at their table.

He stood when he saw her and immediately knew something was wrong with her. He asked her if everything was okay and Melissa said that everything was fine. Jeremiah knew that something was wrong, but she wasn't ready to talk about it right now.

Jeremiah asked if she had ever eaten here before and that the steak was amazing here? Melissa told him that she trusted him in ordering for her and that she loved steak and wasn't picky at all. He ordered their food and then jumped in talking about the building that was across the street. Melissa told him that the location was in a great spot and that they had a price drop on it a few months ago. Jeremiah told her that he had purchased the building and wanted to see what the best product would be to go with to furnishing it and getting it ready.

Melissa and Jeremiah talked business for a while and then the food came, and they took a break to eat. The food was good, but Jeremiah couldn't help but to see sadness in Melissa's eyes. Melissa excused herself to the restroom and Jeremiah watched her walk away.

Melissa went to the restroom and all that she could think about was whether this was Jeff's first time or not, did he really love her or not and how could he do something like this after all the things that she put up from him? Not realizing it Melissa was losing her cool. She figured that she needed to get herself together before this business deal turned out bad.

She wiped her tears away and went back to the table. Jeremiah was ending a phone call and stood when she got back out. Jeremiah also had a master's degree in psychology and knew when he needed to say something. He let her know that this is not about business, but she can be open with him and that he wouldn't judge her, but he was there to listen. He let her know that he was also a therapist and that she could have a free session.

Melissa was amazed and knew that she should try to talk with someone else. She told him everything that she had just gone through and that she was very hurt because she loved her husband, but she couldn't trust him now. Jeremiah listened and then told her that the first thing she should do was to take the rest of the day off because she needed time to process the situation.

Melissa called her job and let them know that she was going to take the rest of the day off for a mental day and that she would see them on Monday. Jeremiah was also on the phone holding his appointments to Monday. When he was done, he asked her if she was finished eating because they were going to go into a more private setting which was at his work office. He gave Melissa the address and said to come straight there.

Melissa agreed and was glad that she was finally getting therapy. She knew that she had asked God for the signs, but she didn't see that he would use a stranger to help her.

When Melissa got to the office, she realized that she had done research on this office because she wanted her and her husband to come to the couple's counseling here. The signs were already there but she didn't know how close they were.

When she walked in Jeremiah was waiting at the front desk talking to a lady who seemed to be his assistant. He let her know to hold the rest of his appointments for today and that he was not to be bothered while he was in this therapy session. They walked down a long hall and went into an office that looked very comfortable.

Jeremiah led her in and told her to get comfortable. He let her know that he could be trusted and that she needed to be completely honest so that her therapy would be effective. He wanted her to start at the beginning.

She told him that they had been married for three years and that she had never been with another man before. She told him that everything was going fine at first until she realized that he would talk to his mother about everything in their relationship, and that he had problems with trying to keep a job. She also told him that he has an addiction to playing video games and he was having a hard time growing up. She told him that she had been putting her dreams aside from being a psychologist because she didn't have the right support and didn't want to complicate things anymore. She also told him about her fear of not being a mother one day because she was in her 30's and it never seemed like the right time.

He listened to every word while writing things down so that he could ask questions when the time was right. Jeremiah asked her about how the betrayal made her feel and what emotions was she feeling right now? Jeremiah was a real good listener, and he definitely knew how to do his job. By the time Melissa finished she had learned how to deal with her emotions and realized what her next steps were.

Jeremiah was helping her, but he was also healing himself. He had a bad breakup where his girlfriend also wasn't faithful. He was able to listen to her situation and learn some tactics that may work for him too. He was also a person trying to do things right by God and realized that God will use your bad and make it good. He was realizing now that he had wasted his time on someone who wanted to date him for his money and not his heart. He knew that helping someone else would also help himself.

Hours later Melissa and Jeremiah had become the best of friends. They were laughing and had shared things they liked and didn't like in relationships. They realized that they had a lot in common. Their birthdays were both in December, they were both in their thirties with no children. They were both career driven and had dreams and also realized that both of them ran track in high school and college.

Jeremiah hadn't ever had a friend like Melissa that was so open and not judgmental. He knew that he wanted to talk with her again because he didn't know what he was missing until he met her.

Melissa got back home, and reality hit her that her husband was not there. She had gotten a message from him letting her know that he would be at his mother's house so she knew that she could spend a little time with the Lord. Melissa put on her worship music and opened her word of God. She knew that she needed some guidance in what to do next because she knew how the enemy would throw good worldly things at her in this vulnerable time with her husband.

Melissa stayed in prayer and worship for about an hour and felt that she had a calming peace in her heart. She realized that everyone had something that they were battling with in their flesh, however she knew that she didn't let the flesh overpower her spirit. Melissa knew after spending time with God that playing the same game as him was not what she wanted to do so she had planned to continue getting some therapy and making sure that she was going to fight with the right weapons and not open another door to anything until that one was closed. She also knew that she had been with him for three years, and not having him there made her wonder if they had gotten married too fast?

She remembered when they were in church one Sunday and she approached him, and he didn't approach her. She was now wondering if she was the one being too pushy or selfish because she knew that she wasn't getting any younger and one day she wanted to be a mother. Melissa thought that she would continue to pray for God to give her the right answers so she decided that she would let the situation play out with time and what was meant to happen would eventually happen.

Melissa thought she would make the best of her weekend since it was Friday, and she had already taken a mental day for today, meaning that she had the weekend alone to do some thinking about her life and where it was going.

Melissa was in the middle of planning her

weekend when her phone rang and it was her husband, Jeff. She took a deep breath and answered the phone. Jeff was saying that he wanted to meet somewhere and talk more. He was saying that he was sorry about how things had happened and that he should not have been so weak in his flesh. He mentioned that he and his mother were talking about it and she said that he was in the wrong and needed to try to make it right in his marriage.

Melissa listened to him and thought that maybe face to face talking would be a good idea because she wanted to make sure he knew that she forgave him and because she would like to move on even if it was not with him. She wanted him to be happy and the best he could be in Christ. Melissa knew that she wouldn't be mad for long, that she just needed time with the Lord. Melissa agreed to meet him for breakfast in the morning so that they could talk about their next steps in their marriage.

Melissa thought that she would go out and get some dinner because she didn't even take anything out to cook. She ordered Texas Roadhouse and went to pick it up at the restaurant. She pulled up and parked in one of the to-go parking spots and called them to let them know that she was outside to pick up her food.

Melissa loved their steaks, so she ordered a 12oz. Ribeye, with a loaded baked potato and broccoli. They had some of the best bread ever, so she made sure she got some of the bread with the sweet butter to top off her meal. They were out in no time to bring her meal. She tipped the girl and pulled off.

When she got home her phone rang and it was her husband. He was asking if he could come tonight and that way they could ride together. Melissa told him that she would rather meet him there and she didn't think it would be a good idea because she didn't want to confuse where they stood at the moment.

Jeff understood and said that he couldn't wait to see her in the morning. Melissa decided to eat and then get into a book called *Rips, Tips and Scripts* by a new local artist named Tamelia Keaton. She heard that the book was a must read for every woman no matter where you were in being a woman. She grabbed the book and got her read on.

An hour later, Melissa had almost finished the book, and it was very powerful. This book was for every woman, and it left Melissa in a deep thought of where she fit in in the story.

It was getting late so Melissa decided to take her bath to relax her a little more, talk to the Lord and put on her relaxing music so that she could fall asleep. It didn't take long at all before Melissa was dreaming of being on a beach relaxing on the sand and drinking a frozen smoothie and enjoying reading a book.

Melissa was awakened by the sunshine beaming in her room and the chirping and talking of the birds. She got up out of the bed, fell on her knees and prayed thanking God for being who he was and taking time to look after her. She and her husband decided that breakfast at 9 would be good and decided on a little family-owned spot that served good breakfast but was not that crowded.

Melissa got up to go into the bathroom to take her shower and get her clothes on. She decided on a pair of khaki dress pants, a tank top and a long sleeve sweater that was black and khaki color. She put on a pair of dress flats and decided that she would let her hair be natural. Melissa didn't wear a lot of makeup only for occasions, so it didn't take her that long to get dressed.

It was about 8:30 so she decided to leave which would put her about 10 minutes earlier than 9. Melissa wasn't late for anything. She was always early for work, paying bills before the due dates and if she had to be somewhere she would be 10 minutes earlier than when she was scheduled.

Melissa was raised by a strong, single mother who knew what she wanted and didn't play any games with anybody about her girls. She had four daughters and all of them were very successful and were either married or had a steady relationship. Her mother raised them with the fear of God and that you always have your own and never depend on a man to support you. Her mother was strong, who also had five strong sisters who were about their business as well.

Melissa loved the relationship that her mother had with her sisters and how they would not hold their tongue for anyone. If you were wrong or weak they would tell you. Melissa's mother was never a person to make decisions for her daughter but it didn't stop her from putting her opinions in if something wasn't right. Melissa remembered when she told her mother that she was getting married to Jeff and her mother went straight in asking what he do for work and how long were they dating? When Melissa told her mother that they were only dating for about 8 months her mother told her that they were moving too fast and that maybe he needed steady income before trying to be someone's husband.

Melissa thought about the past and realized that she didn't pray about it long enough and was too blinded on seeing that maybe she would be too old to be a mother one day. Melissa thought it would be best to find out what she and her husband were going to decide to do before letting her mother in. One thing that she knew was that when you get married, even if you loved your family, they didn't need to be all in your relationship.

She had wished that Jeff would listen to the word of God because his mother was always in the middle of everything they did in their marriage. She reminded herself that if it was ever going to work he was going to have to start putting things in order with the word of God because she married him and not his mother.

Melissa pulled up at 15 minutes till 9 and saw Jeff's truck out front. He was never on time for anything unless it had something to do with a video game. He was late on birthdays and anniversaries, and he was always running late for work. Tardiness was one of the reasons why he couldn't keep a good job which also led to attendance issues.

She thought about how he had been portrayed as the perfect guy and now three years later she could see his weaknesses which had now led their relationship to a new struggle that she didn't know he had. She didn't even know he was drinking and now that he was battling with being faithful to her. Melissa started blaming herself and trying to understand what would cause him to do this.

She thought back on what Jeremiah said in the therapy session that she could not blame herself because her husband was the one who made the decisions. Melissa thought that she would make sure that she would at least ask her husband about it and so that they could at least get some closure in the struggle.

She walked in and noticed that Jeff was already holding a table in the back of the restaurant. When he saw her, he stood up and started to meet her so that he could lead her back to the table. He kissed her on the cheek which made Melissa feel a little awkward. Jeff realized that he had made her a little uncomfortable, so he apologized for it. Melissa told him that it was ok, but she was still trying to understand why he did it. Jeff seemed very hurt and told her that he was having a weak moment.

The waitress came to the table, and she was very pretty. Melissa watched as Jeff gave her a long stare and a friendly smile. Melissa watched their eye contact, and it was speaking as if they knew each other already or maybe wanting to know each other later.

Melissa cleared her throat to get her husband's attention and Jeff was looking very embarrassed that he got caught staring at the waitress. The waitress' name was Krystal and Melissa thought how there were so many women who are so unhappy with themselves that they would even try to get with someone's husband even when the wife was there. Melissa thought about the author and understood why she was writing the book because the world was different, and it needed some help starting with the women.

Melissa and Jeff ordered their food, and the waitress took their menus and went off to get their drinks. Melissa asked about his family and were they all doing ok. Jeff said that his family were all good and that they were going to the beach next month. Melissa wanted to just make cordial conversations giving their food time to come back and they wouldn't be interrupted.

About 15 minutes later, the waitress came back with their food and made sure they didn't need any condiments before she left. Melissa let them know that they were ok and thanked her for bringing the food so quickly. She gave Melissa a smile and looked back at Jeff before walking away.

Melissa and Jeff blessed the food and decided to get a bite to eat. The food was very well prepared, and Melissa seemed very hungry this morning. She was eating her food when she noticed that Jeff was staring at her and not eating his food. Melissa asked him if the food was ok and Jeff said that he didn't have much of an appetite. Melissa watched as Jeff's eyes were wandering around in the restaurant and finally landed on the waitress. Melissa stopped eating and asked Jeff if he knew her.

Jeff was caught off guard because he didn't see

that his wife was watching him watch her. This made Melissa feel that she was wasting her time. She told her husband that he must be so far away from God because he couldn't even see how disrespectful he was being especially after what they had been through recently. Jeff made excuses that he only wanted her, and Melissa felt that to heal and forgive completely she needed to face it and talk with him about it. She told him how he allowed the enemy to come into their relationship, and he had always had a door open by always letting his mother in on everything that was going on in their relationship.

Jeff seemed frustrated when she mentioned his mother, but it didn't stop her. Melissa told him that she couldn't trust him after the incident and if there is no trust there is nothing left. Jeff explained that he wanted to go to counseling because he felt off somewhere.

Melissa encouraged him to go to counseling because she was doing the same. Melissa told Jeff about Jeremiah and how she had started seeing him as her therapist. Jeff seemed a little jealous, but he didn't say anything. Melissa told him that she was willing to work with the mother boy issues and the financial issues, but she couldn't deal with him cheating on her.

Melissa, while having breakfast with her husband, realized that her husband had allowed the enemy to get into their marriage and now he was allowing temptation to lead him into sin. Melissa knew that she was going to have to stay prayed up and that some things only come by fasting and praying and she would do both.

She was walking into her home when she

received a phone call from Jeremiah who was wanting to get her on the schedule for Monday. Melissa asked him if he would have something on Tuesday instead because she knew that she would need Monday to get caught up from the two days that she took off. Jeremiah put her down for 12 p.m. on Tuesday and they said their goodbyes until later.

Melissa knew that she was going to relax the rest of the weekend. She called her massage therapist along with her pedicure and manicure spot and made an appointment for later on so that she wouldn't have to wait. She still had a couple of hours before leaving, so she thought that she would get into the Word a little so that she could get some answers on what God was telling her about her relationship, as well as the new struggles that she was having with her husband.

She realized that Jeff was a little disrespectful at breakfast date and he was clearly flirting with the waitress right in front of her even after he just slept with another woman. Melissa just needed him to know that she still loved him and that she had forgiven him for what he did. The question now was whether she would be able to move past the situation and trust him again as her husband. She weighed the struggles that she already had in him not being a responsible man, and now the new struggles of not trusting him.

Melissa knew that God would give her the next steps to follows and that He would fix the situation, but she also knew that sometimes God doesn't fix things the way we want him to fix them. Melissa opened the word and started reading the book of Ephesians and was finding out a lot on order of the household. About an hour later Melissa drifted off into a peaceful sleep holding the word of God.

Melissa woke up and it was about an hour before her appointment to get her manicure and pedicure. When she finished with that, she would go to the massage parlor so she could experience total relaxation. She went to get dressed and figured she might leave earlier to beat the traffic at this time of the day. Both places were in the downtown area so she wouldn't have to do a lot to walk from the parking lot so that she would be on time for her appointment.

She walked in and was greeted by her technician and was able to get right into the seat to get waited on. She noticed that there were quite a few people waiting but that was the benefit of making the appointment.

She was soaking her feet and thinking and then Jeremiah came to her mind. She thought about how much they had in common and how he went through a similar situation like herself. She thought about how he was set and steady in his career like herself and that he was so easy to talk with. She knew that it wouldn't be Christ like to open anything right now while she was still trying to heal while still loving her husband and being portrayed.

Jeremiah seemed very easy to talk with and never tried to take her from her husband or make him even look bad. It was like talking with a female best friend while offering good sound advice. She knew that she would have to tread lightly on this because she also knew that the enemy would send what you wanted to trick you to get you off track. She made up her mind that she would fast and pray so that she could be clear on what her next move would be and to be sure that she would not move until God told her to. She would fast and pray not just for herself but for her husband to desire the Lord more and so that he could come out victorious in his own struggles.

Melissa finished about an hour in a half later, paid for her services, tipped her technician and left to go back to her car. She came out the door and was walking towards the parking deck when she thought that she saw someone familiar. The more she saw him the more it confirmed that it was her husband. She heard him talking with a female and as she was walking to her car, she saw the waitress and her husband out in public having a drink and eating dessert.

Melissa was boiling inside but knew that she needed to carry herself like a child of God. Melissa walked up to her husband and politely interrupted. Jeff saw his wife and almost jumped as if he had seen a ghost. Melissa looked at the woman and saw that her head was down as if she was embarrassed about knowing what she had done was wrong. Melissa eased both of their fears and let her husband know that she had made her decision with where they stood in their relationship and that she had prayed for him and she was going to put it into God's hands.

Melissa told the waitress that she should be ashamed of herself and that she needed to wait for God to send her a Godsent man and not a man that belongs to someone else because she was a beautiful young lady that deserved to be first in a man's life. The woman apologized and told Jeff that she didn't want to see him anymore.

Jeff lost twice because Melissa then told him that he needed to get closer to Christ and get some help. Melissa told her husband that they would continue to live separately until she got what God wanted her to do. Her feelings were done with him, and she wanted a divorce to move on with her life, however the spirit was telling her not yet and time would tell it all. She listened to the spirit and decided to make it to her massage appointment. She knew that she really needed to relax after what she had just experienced.

Melissa was very relaxed when she came out of the massage parlor and was ready to pray, and got in bed early so that she could make it to church tomorrow. She loved church but realized that she wasn't ready to face Jeff and his mother in the situation. She thought maybe finding another church was also needed so that she could start detaching from everything that was tied to him.

She had heard of this church that had a great ministry, and the Pastor and First Lady were all about the Kingdom's business. The name was New Life International Church, and they were all out supporting the community. The Pastor was a great man of God, and his wife was a great saint and a good example for the women. They were a powerful couple for the Lord. She had met them at an outreach event where they had sponsored a wellness fair and was encouraging a healthier life which included eating right, working out doing Zumba with Dwaine and the event was in a cool place called The MEC.

Melissa had picked up a pamphlet and a care package and said that she would one day visit their church because all the women with these leaders were very nice and extended the heart of God. She thought that this might be the best time to visit the location and to see how the church service was, and it would keep her in church but give her the time needed to be able to deal with her husband and his family.

Melissa went into her home and decided to order in for dinner so that she could continue to get ready for Sunday morning. She went and found the pamphlet and noticed that New Life's church service started at 10AM. She noticed that it was about a 30-minute drive from where she was because the church was in East Spencer which was about 10 minutes from Salisbury.

She heard a knock on the door and realized that her food had arrived. She went to the door to get her food, tipped the driver and went to the bedroom. She was sitting in her chair and thought that she would finish the book that she was reading. She noticed that this book was good for every woman, and she even realized that it gave her some insights about her current situation.

After she finished eating, she went to get ready for bed because her body was certainly very relaxed and it wouldn't take her long to drift off to sleep. She put on her relaxing music and fell into a deep sleep which was much needed at this moment.

Melissa was awakened when she thought that she heard someone come into the house. It was about 3 a.m. and she wasn't expecting anyone. She grabbed a robe and grabbed her pepper spray and bat from the closet. There was someone in the house because she heard something moving around in the kitchen.

Melissa began to pray as she tiptoed to the door and slightly opened it to see what she could see. She could see a shadow, but it was dark, and she couldn't see if it was her husband or not. She was grabbing her phone to call the police when the light in the kitchen came on and she saw that it was her husband.

She yelled at him and asked him why he would scare her like that. Jeff had clearly been drinking and had used his key to come back into the house. He was slurring his words, and he seemed to not understand where he was at.

Melissa grabbed him and he tried to hug her and kiss her. Melissa broke the embrace and told him that he needed to lay down and sleep it off. She went to grab him a blanket and pillow and came back to find Jeff already sleeping on the couch. She covered him up and went to check the front door to ensure it was locked and then went back into her bedroom, shut the door and fell back to sleep.

She wasn't glad that Jeff had made his way back to their house after she had told him to stay away but she thanked God that it wasn't a real intruder coming in to do her any harm. She fell back to sleep so that she could get up to go to the new church in the morning.

Melissa woke up and noticed that it was already

morning. The time was 6:33 a.m. and she noticed that she heard Jeff moving around in the kitchen. She knew that he wasn't trying to cook anything because he didn't do that when she even needed him to.

Melissa got out of bed and put on some jogging pants and a long-sleeved shirt so she could see what all the commotion was about in the kitchen. She opened her door and found that Jeff was trying to prepare her some breakfast. He greeted her with a good morning and an apology for waking her up so soon.

Melissa sat down and asked him if he needed any help so he wouldn't burn down the house. Jeff and Melissa both laughed, and he said that he could handle it. Melissa knew why she fell for Jeff because he looked so innocent and was very well put together. When she first married him, he portrayed to be everything she needed and wanted in a husband. She was reminiscing about all the good times they had together and the reasons why she just knew it would work out. But then the bad times came to mind and all the issues they just had to endure in the last couple of weeks, and she remembered why they were in this predicament now.

Melissa was in deep thought that she didn't hear her husband call her name and ask her if she wanted her eggs scrambled or boiled. Melissa answered boiled and thanked Jeff for trying to be considerate. Jeff continued to cook the meat and do the toast so that they could eat together.

About twenty minutes later the breakfast was done and they were eating and talking about what was next in their relationship. Melissa told Jeff that she felt totally disrespected and that he made choices that helped her to make a decision because of his actions he took in the last couple of weeks. Jeff seemed to look confused and sad at the same time.

Melissa got up to give him a hug and told him that she would always love him, but she was going to have to heal from all of this which included continuing her therapy with Jeremiah. Jeff seemed to understand and said that he needed to get some counseling as well because he was dealing with a stronghold of not being able to leave other women alone and the desire to want to drink alcohol because of the way it made him feel.

Melissa suggested that he get some help so that he could heal because she knew that God could help him through it all. Jeff said that he wanted to go to church together and that his mother wanted to talk with her. Melissa let him know that she was going to visit this new church because they were so involved with the community and they already had a connection with her. Melissa let Jeff know that she wasn't going to make any fast decisions unless God wanted her to. Jeff started to cry and said that he wasn't being completely honest with her about the situation.

Jeff told Melissa that the waitress that he was with was the same girl that he had slept with at his friend's house and that they had been in a relationship for about three months. He also told her that it was his fault because she didn't know that he was married. He would take his ring off and tell her lies. Jeff was honest to tell her that when they were at the restaurant, he told her that she was his sister so that he could continue to see her on the side. He admitted that after the last date, when Melissa talked to her about how she shouldn't want to be second, touched her and after the incident the girl left him alone and said that she never wanted to see him anymore.

Melissa sat with a shocked look on her face and realized that her husband was just not cheating but having an affair on her. Part of her was sad but the other part was glad that he was being honest with her. Melissa cried and said that she forgave him and thanked him for being honest with her, but she was not able to be with him. She told him that she would like to get a divorce. She let him know that when he decided to make their relationship 3 instead of 2 he broke the vows with the Lord and her, and it would be hard to trust him again.

She recommended that he get some help so that he can get back to being his best self with the Lord so that his soul could get right. Melissa said that she would get the lawyer to draw up the separation document and she handed Jeff back her wedding rings. Melissa wanted to possibly make her marriage work but realized that she had been the only one in it.

Melissa told Jeff that she would be changing the locks and there was no reason that they should see each other again. She let him know that the attorney would be getting in touch with him about the property and what their next steps would be. Jeff apologized to her and told her that he never meant to hurt her and that he wouldn't make this a hard process with settling things.

Melissa was heartbroken and said her thanks and led him to the door to let him out. They hugged each other one last time and Melissa knew that would be the last hug.

Melissa knew that this was a trick of the enemy to try to keep her out of church, so she decided that it wasn't going to happen. She went into her room to get her some church clothes so that she could leave at a decent time to get there by 10. She needed God right now because this weekend had been far from relaxing and she already needed to do a redo.

She jumped in the shower and thought about all the things Jeff had said to her and thanked God that he told her the truth now and not later when she decided to take him back or start a family with him. God worked in mysterious ways that he didn't allow her to bring a child into this world in these conditions. A big part of her wanted to stay in her marriage but the other part of her knew that her husband was dealing with some struggles that only God could help him with. Only time would tell but for now she needed to get in the presence of God so that she could ensure her mind would stay on Him.

Melissa finished dressing, locked her door and hopped in the car heading down to New Life International Church where she knew that God would meet her there.

The ride to the church was about 30 minutes, which wasn't that long at all. It was in East Spencer on Heilingtown Road. When she walked in they were doing the morning prayer, and she could already feel the anointing when she walked on the church grounds. The service was great, and they even cited a God-given confidence statement that empowered her to always love and believe in herself and not to let anyone control her. The word that was given from the Pastor was awesome and she was able to take some good notes to be able to study it later as well.

When the service was almost over the Pastor called her up and said that he wanted the women to pray with her. She was surprised that she was even noticed because there was barely anywhere to sit in the church. When she got to the altar the pastor told her that even though it is rough right now to stay in her God safe place.

Melissa knew that this was God meeting her where she was because she didn't know anyone at this church. He told her that God was a redeemer of time and not to feel that she did anything wrong. Melissa needed a word, and she got what she came for. The ladies prayed a powerful prayer over her life and Melissa left the altar feeling like a brand-new person.

After the service was over plenty of people came to hug her and thanked her for coming to worship with them and to come back soon. They took her number and information and said that someone would be in touch with her. Melissa knew that she would be coming back to visit because God was in that location.

Melissa knew that she must stay prayed-up because after getting a word like that the enemy was coming to try to steal it and he was going to have a fight on his hands. Melissa stopped and got her something to eat at a soul food place called Taste of the Triad where you could get nothing but the best southern soul food in the city. The staff was always nice, and the food would never leave you disappointed. She went home and decided to finish the book and relax so that she could go back to work energized on Monday morning.

She knew that she had a lot of big decisions to make so she was going to start fasting so that she could make sure she was making the right decisions, but she knew for sure that she was going to get the separation papers done by her attorney first thing Monday morning.

One Year Later...

Melissa walked out of the court a free woman. She was glad that Jeff and she were still cordial with one another even though he and his mistress decided to give things another shot. Melissa and she were also okay, and the girl was able to apologize for how things went down in the beginning because Jeff didn't tell her that they were married.

One thing Melissa knew was that you must forgive everyone so that you can move on and nobody will have power over you. Melissa was still receiving counseling from Jeremiah's coworker because Jeremiah and Melissa had become great friends, and it was getting awkward at the counseling sessions. Jeremiah had a girlfriend who Melissa had become very close to, and they all were hanging out like they knew each other for years.

Melissa had decided to put her resignation in at Jeff's church and join New Life International Church because she was getting the right teaching at that location and it was also a way to not make things awkward at Jeff and his mother's church. Melissa sold the house that they had and split the profit since they got it together and both kept their own car.

Melissa was offered another position at the bank which involved her assisting fifteen branches with ensuring that they were ready for bank audits, which was a lot of responsibility and very exciting. She bought another house in the Kannapolis area, which was also closer to the church she joined, and she was also working with the finance team at church. Life was good and she had never felt so free.

Word got around real fast at church that she was not married and that she was a very successful businesswoman so there were plenty of men who were trying to take her out. Melissa wasn't looking but she knew that if God wanted it to happen it would, but she would just take her time.

There was an assistant pastor who was very attractive who seemed to be interested in her, but she would just wait on God. He tried to take her out a couple of times, but Melissa let him know that she had just got out of a marriage, and didn't want to rush into anything too fast. He understood and said that he would wait but he knew what the Lord had already told him about her.

Melissa knew that she would verify that, and she just kept doing what she was supposed to do. Melissa did think about it and realized that she was in her 30's and did want to raise a family but she would not make the same mistake that she had made with Jeff.

For now, she would keep God first, excel in her job and continue to serve in her church. Melissa knew that if she continued to seek God and his righteousness other things that she wanted would be added to her so she didn't worry about when it would happen, she just knew that one day it would.

THE END

ABUSE STRUGGLES

Teresa was awakened by her husband dragging her off the couch, yelling at her about not sleeping with him in bed last night. She braced herself for whatever her husband was going to do next, which would normally involve using her as his punching bag and then tossing her around like an old rag doll. Teresa tried to beg him to stop but the rage in his face showed that she would have to take his wrath.

Teresa drifted off into her safe place where she imagined having life before he started to put his hands on her. Her husband was named Charles, and he had a history of putting his hands on a female. Charles came from a generation of men who didn't like to be challenged and wanted to put their hands on females to get power and control.

Teresa said her prayers silently and prayed to God that this wouldn't be her last time on earth. It seemed like eternity, but she came back to realization when she noticed that she was lying on the floor without any of her clothes on and her husband was getting up off her pulling up his pants.

This was at least a once-a-week thing where she would go through these incidents and he would also take what he wanted from her and leave her with the shame of feeling confused, scared, hurt and disgusted.

Why couldn't she just leave? She didn't have any

children, thank God, but she seemed to feel that one day he would change and realize that his behavior was hurting her. That one day needed to come soon because it was now four years later and she was still going through the same behavior.

Teresa wondered what she did wrong to get this type of treatment from the person who claimed he loved her. She remembered when Charles and she had just started dating. They were high school lovers and inseparable. He would always shower her with gifts, love and even write her poems. He never showed any signs of being an abuser and she was so in love with him. Her friends at school and other people envied her because he would always treat her like a queen by opening her car doors and showering her with expensive gifts. She had never had anyone to treat her like that before and knew that she one day wanted Charles to be her husband.

When they graduated from high school, she had a full scholarship to go to St. Augustine College in Raleigh. But Charles went to Winston Salem State University and told her that she should stay in Winston so that he could protect her. Her mother, sisters and friends tried to talk her into following her dreams, saying that if he really loved her that he would also want her to pursue her dreams as well and would wait on her.

Teresa didn't listen and decided to go to Winston Salem State University to be close to Charles. Teresa enjoyed staying on campus and she was doing very well in her classes. She had met a couple of new friends and had started to get used to college campus life.

On the other hand, Charles was playing football and had started to change a little because he was a star on the field, which attracted the attention of some females which he was liking a little too much. Teresa noticed that Charles and she were getting a little distant and that he was hanging out too much. Charles' grades started to decline due to him hanging out having too much fun with his friends.

Teresa had started to notice when other guys showed a little interest in her Charles was ready to fight, which caused problems in their relationship. Teresa let Charles know that maybe they should take a break so that he could get himself together and decide on whether they were going to stay in a relationship or not. Charles agreed and immediately started to see another girl at the school to try to make her jealous.

Teresa continued to do well in college and hung out with her own friends. Charles and she stayed friends even though he had moved on with the other girl. She still loved Charles so she may have gone on a couple of dates but none of them were serious enough to pursue. Even though Teresa was hurt, she stayed focused on what was important, which was school and herself. Teresa had a strong faith in God and had decided that no matter what, she was going to wait to give herself to her husband and to stay right with the Lord.

Teresa decided that she would join the college's dance team, which took up a lot more of her time when she wasn't studying. The college was known for being a black college and being about their business when it came to showing up for games, special events and Homecoming.

She and Charles had become distant, and he was still going strong with his new girlfriend. Charles was barely keeping his grades up, so as a result, he was put off the football team for not keeping a high enough average GPA to stay on the team. This made him very upset, and he started drinking more to keep his image.

Teresa had heard around the college that Charles had put his hands on his girlfriend, and he was reported, which caused him to be put off the campus. He went into a depression and called Teresa to talk with her. Teresa was a friend to everyone, so she just listened to him talk about what was going on with him. Charles mentioned that he didn't want to be like his father and that he was thinking about getting some counseling to help him deal with some childhood issues that wouldn't stop haunting him.

Teresa told him that would be a great idea and that he still had time to get it right and to get back into college. Charles told her that he should have stayed with her and that she was the only girl that he had ever loved. Teresa let him know that she loved him too, but he needed to get some help. They ended the conversation with Teresa, agreeing that they may start over if he keeps his word with getting some professional help. Charles never got any counseling.

Teresa and Charles started dating again anyway and everything was going well. They had agreed that they were going to take things slow because she was very busy with school and being a dancer. Homecoming was coming up and they had to be in the parade, and she knew that she would have to practice a lot while studying.

Charles told her that he loved her and that he would wait until she was ready. He let her know that he would support her and come to the parade to support her. He was not able to come on campus again because of the incident but when they were at away games, he would come to support her. Everything was going well at first.

Teresa was very attractive so everywhere she went men would look her way. It didn't help that she danced for WSSU, and she was a really good dancer so she was always noticed by others.

Homecoming week came and it was quite fun. She had to participate in different activities including a step show. There was something going on every day of the week up to the parade and game on Saturday, so Teresa stayed involved in the activities. She was living the college dream.

She noticed that Charles was beginning to act jealous when she was not with him all the time. They would have arguments, and she would always have to explain to him that she wanted to be with him and nobody else. Charles began to get a little clingy where he wanted to go everywhere she went, which was a problem because he couldn't be on campus because of his actions.

Charles came from a well-off household where he was the only child. His mother was very submissive, and his father was a little controlling, but he provided well for his family. Charles's parents loved Teresa because they knew she came from a Christian household and that she was trying to honor God, which meant not trying to move too fast.

Charles would notice how men would look at Teresa and even try to take her on dates, but Teresa wouldn't give them a chance because she loved Charles, and in a relationship with only him, but this wasn't enough for Charles. He always wanted to argue about her not needing to be on the campus without him and that she and he should move into an apartment together.

Teresa had no intentions of moving in with a man and they weren't married so she told him that she wouldn't do it. Charles wasn't happy that she didn't want to do things his way, so he got mad and raised his voice at her in public. Teresa was very embarrassed, and she left him in the restaurant and called for an Uber to pick her up. When she got back to the campus Charles had already called her over five times, which she didn't answer. She thought about how he made her feel and felt that maybe this relationship needed to be over. She thought about what they had been through and how good it was in high school. She wanted to go back in time and get the old Charles because she didn't know who this new one was, and she didn't like him at all.

She decided to go with some of her dancing buddies and go to the study hall to get caught up on some work. Teresa walked out of her dorm room and didn't notice that Charles' car was on campus. She walked to her friend's dorm and was about to go in when Charles jumped out of the car and came towards her yelling at her for not answering his phone calls. She looked around at her surroundings and thanked God that nobody was around to hear how he was embarrassing her again.

Teresa tried to make it to her destination when Charles grabbed her arm and pulled her towards him. Teresa yelled that he was hurting her, and Charles snapped back into reality. He embraced her with a hug and told her that he loved her, and he couldn't live without her. He promised that he wouldn't do it again and that he would get help so that he could be the perfect man for her.

Teresa cried in his arms and realized that she didn't know why she couldn't move on and why she loved him so much. They walked back to Charle's car and talked about the two incidents and Charles was in tears apologizing for his mess ups. Teresa forgave him and Charles got out to walk around to her side of the car.

When he opened the door, he fell on his knees and asked her to marry him. The ring was very well picked out. Teresa looked at Charles and was going to tell him that it was too soon, but Charles told her that it doesn't have to be right now, but he wanted to make sure that she was all his. Teresa knew that she didn't love anyone else, so she told him yes.

She knew after what they just went through she should run away and never look back, but she thought that everyone deserves a second chance and with counseling she just knew that he would make a great husband. Charles told her that his father bought him a condo, and they were furnishing it and that whenever she was ready, she would always have a place to stay.

Teresa told him that she was going to stay on campus, which wasn't the answer that Charles wanted to hear, but he held his rage in because he didn't want to do anything else to make her say no to his proposal. Charles knew that if he made her his wife, he could get her to do what he wanted her to do because he knew that she was going to honor those wedding vows to God no matter what. Charles wanted her in every single way, and he was getting very impatient on how long she was making him wait. He was a selfish person but he knew how to play on her emotions. Love to him meant her giving him everything he wanted because she was all his and nobody else's.

Three Years Later....

Teresa couldn't believe that she was walking across the college stage, graduating with her bachelor's in education. Her family and Charle's family were there to support her. Charles and she had been holding strong and had set a date in six months for their wedding. Her mother thought that it was too fast, but she was always going to support her daughter because she knew that she had raised her daughter right.

Charles's family was pressuring her to move into the condo so that Charles could take care of her, however she told them until she was married that she would stay with her parents until after the wedding day. Charles and she were holding strong, and he had gone and completed some counseling to help him with some of his rage and childhood issues.

Charles was constantly rushing her to become his wife and even asked if she wanted to elope and get it over with. Teresa told him that she wanted a church wedding, and she wanted her friends and family to be a part of the wedding. Charles wanted her to have what she wanted so he waited until the wedding.

Six months later the wedding was here and gone and she was now married to Charles. For the first year everything was perfect but afterwards she started seeing how he was getting very controlling and embarrassing her more in front of people, mainly in public. When she tried to talk with him about it, he mentioned that she was his wife and that she needed to respect him more. He would always bring up how she was supposed to be more submissive.

Teresa noticed that every time she would talk with him about a job in her field, he would make excuses of why she needed to stay at home, and he would provide for her. He was a great provider and had gone back to school to get his engineering degree in electronics and landed a job that made six figures a year.

Teresa wanted to utilize her degree as well, but it was always an argument with her husband. Not only did he not want her to work but he started making her change her clothing because he said that it showed too much and too many men were looking at her when they were out in public. Everything Teresa wanted to do or anybody she would hang out with Charles had a problem with. He only wanted to do things his family did and never wanted her to spend any time with her family or friends. Teresa started to feel alone and thought it was time to have a conversation with her husband.

Teresa thought it would be best to cook her husband's favorite dinner which was fried chicken, mac and cheese and broccoli. Charles loved her cooking and if she got into the right mood she loved to cook for him. She knew that when he got off after 6p he would be ready to eat a good home cooked meal. Teresa turned her gospel music on and got into the kitchen to do her thing. She had about another hour before her husband got off of work, so she wanted to make sure everything was good and hot for him.

Time flies when you were having fun and it wasn't long before she heard the key turn in the door and her husband was walking into the house. She spoke to him from the kitchen, and he came in and hugged her from the back, turned her around and kissed her on the forehead. Teresa turned down her music and asked her husband how his day was. Charles told her that it was very busy but productive and he couldn't wait to eat her dinner. She smiled and told him to go get cleaned up and the dinner would be ready in about ten minutes.

Teresa was going over how she would say things in her head about him being a little overprotective and that she wanted to pursue getting her master's degree in psychology, which was her original dream of getting her doctorate degree in psychology. She loved her husband and appreciated how he provided for her, however he was making a big deal when she decided to do anything that she wanted to do. She was losing her reality and what she wanted to do.

Charles came back down and sat at the table and watched while his wife fixed their plates and drinks and served him like he liked to be served. He loved a wife that he could take care of and spoil as long as she did things his way. Teresa sat the plates on the table and took her seat so that they could bless the food together. Charles said the grace and they were both eating when Charles started to talk with Teresa about him wanting to start a family. Teresa put her head down and thought that it was now or never to have this conversation with her husband.

Teresa looked at her husband and told him that one day she would love to start a family, but she would also like to get her doctorate degree first and get into her career first, so they would be more stable together. Charles looked at her as if he wasn't pleased with her answer. Teresa could feel a shift in the room, so she tried to rub his hands to calm him down. She let Charles know that she had felt alone at home and that he had alienated her away from her friends and family. She let him know that the only family that comes around was his family and that she wanted to be able to see her family as well. Teresa mentioned that lately he had been a little controlling when they were out in public and had even started making a big deal of what she could wear and not wear in public. Teresa let him know that she loved the fact that he spoiled her and bought some of her clothes but that she wanted to be able to go out and buy her own clothes sometimes.

Charles immediately stood up and started yelling at

her for being ungrateful for everything that he did for her. Teresa immediately regretted telling him anything. He stood up and before Teresa could protect herself, he punched her in her face and then grabbed her by her neck and started choking her where she couldn't breathe.

Teresa tried to fight back but the weight that he had on her was impossible to move. Teresa had seen him angry, but he had never hit her before. Teresa was gagging for air and had almost blanked out for a lack of oxygen when Charles realized that he was almost about to kill his wife. He snapped back into reality and immediately started to apologize about hitting her and that he wouldn't do it again.

He reached out to try to hug her but Teresa ran to the bedroom in her own thoughts crying and not knowing what to do next. She put the lock on the door and sat on the floor sobbing and thinking about what she should do next. Charles was banging on the door demanding that she let him in, which caused Teresa to go into their bathroom and lock that door as well with her cell phone just in case she had to call the police.

She looked in the mirror only to notice how she had a swollen face and a black eye. She didn't know what she would do to hide her face from anyone because it was very noticeable. She thought about all the times that Charles had raised his voice and grabbed her a few times, but he had never hit her before. What did she say that triggered him? Was it her fault? Teresa had so many questions to try to justify why she was at fault for him giving her a black eye.

On the outside of her bedroom door, she could hear

Charles begging and pleading that he promised that it would be the last time and that he would go back to therapy and he didn't want to be this way. It was his father's fault and how he saw him treat his mother.

Teresa had a very good heart and always wanted to help the hurt kid in anyone, including her husband. She opened the door and went to hug her husband and believed him when he said that he would get help and it wouldn't happen again. Charles carried her to their bedroom, and he went to get her some ice for her eye. He apologized over and over while trying to get the swelling to go down on her face.

Teresa knew that by the way he was taking care of her that he wouldn't do it again because he loved her, right? She didn't know that because she didn't do anything about it or fight back, the situation would only get worse.

Teresa woke up the next morning to the worst headache she had ever had. The swelling was worse, and her face looked like she had just lost a fight with Muhammad Ali. She didn't know if makeup could hide the black eye from anyone. She was so hurt and embarrassed that she decided to just cancel all her outside plans of getting back into school and looking for her dream career right now.

She didn't want to tell her mother because then her mother would be judgmental. She didn't trust telling his family because they would probably take his side. He had already alienated her from all her friends so that was out of the equation. Teresa realized that she was all alone on the earthly side and the only person who would care would be the good Lord above, so she fell on her knees and began to cry out to the only father, friend and God that she could trust. She stayed on her knees praying that God would change the situation. She let him know that she loved her husband and wanted to honor her marriage, but she didn't want to take any more harsh punishment that her husband called love. She cried and cried thanking God even though her situation wasn't where she wanted it to be and then she laid on her face and waited to listen to what the Lord would say to her. After about an hour, she got up with God's peace and his strength to make it through another day.

Teresa went to take a shower and put some clothes on and noticed that she smelled the smell of breakfast cooking in the kitchen. She was nervous that her husband should be at work but was still downstairs cooking breakfast. He never did any cooking so she was almost afraid to eat, especially after the fight they had the night before.

She tried to put a little makeup on her face but light as her complexion was, she was not able to hide the bruise that was on her face. She went downstairs and her husband greeted her at the kitchen door with a hug. She reciprocated the hug even though it was more in fear and then asked him if he needed her to take over. He told her that he had it and that he wanted them to spend the day together to smooth things over from last night. Teresa let out a sigh and was hoping that she could have had the day to think things over on her own while he was a work.

Charles sat their plates on the table and went to the refrigerator to get them some orange juice. Teresa kept her head down a lot because she was embarrassed that he had caused her so much pain. Charles noticed that her eye looked really bad and he constantly kept apologizing for it.

Teresa told him that they really needed help because she was not able to take this type of abuse. Charles mentioned that he would get some help and that it wouldn't happen again. Teresa ate her breakfast in silence and then told Charles she was going back to the bedroom to get some rest because her head was starting to hurt. Charles seemed defeated and tried all he could to help her, but nothing seemed to work. Teresa went upstairs and got in the bed and started to cry more from the emotions she was feeling inside.

She didn't even feel the same way about him since the incident. It was hard to look into his eyes because all she saw was the monster from last night. She knew that God would fix it for her, but she didn't know how or when. She thought about getting her bag and getting away from him, but then she knew that she was supposed to stick and stay in her marriage to honor her vows. She was confused and decided that she would wait for the Lord to give her an answer.

It wasn't long before she was back asleep, having a nightmare of her husband hitting her again, choking her and then having his way with her. She woke up panting and sweating knowing that she would need someone to talk to in person to help her with the healing process.

Charles sat down in the living room thinking about what he did and how he was going to fix it. He didn't know what had come over him and he had never hit his wife before. He sat thinking about all the days he had saw his daddy hit his mother when his dad got mad and told himself that he would never do that to his wife and that he would always protect his mother and, now that he had never forgave his father for violating his mother, he was becoming the person that he couldn't forgive. Charles knew that he needed some real help and if not, it was a generational curse that needed to be broken, especially before he had his own kids.

He went upstairs to see how he could help both with keeping their marriage because he knew that he really loved his wife, but he had a serious problem. He went upstairs only to find his wife in bed, crying and depressed. When he came up, he could tell that she tried to stop crying so that he wouldn't notice. He got in bed beside her and tried to comfort her, but he could feel the fear in her body.

He tried to resist the evil that was building inside of him, and he couldn't. He grabbed her forcefully and yelled at her that he was only trying to help her! This was obviously the wrong move because she got up and ran and locked herself in the bathroom. She yelled that she wanted him to leave until he calmed down because she didn't want him to hurt her anymore. Charles told her that this was his house and that he wasn't going anywhere and that if she didn't come out he was coming in!

Teresa told him that she would leave but wanted

him to give her some time to get some clothes. This really made Charles mad to know that his wife wanted to leave him. He forcefully kept hitting the door trying to get in. He wasn't successful so he went to get a hammer to give him some help. By this time Teresa knew that it would be trouble, so she got on the phone to call the police. Before she could give the address, Charles had got into the bathroom door and grabbed her by her hair and dragged her out to the bedroom.

Teresa kicked and tried to fight back but he was too strong. He smacked her across the face and slung her to the bed. She tried to get away, but he put his weight on top of her while taking off his pants. Teresa knew that he was crazy but knew that she needed to find a safe place to hide. He was choking her and she must have passed out. When she woke up she noticed that her husband was pulling up his pants and getting off her. She noticed that she was missing her underclothes and had been raped by her own husband.

She knew that this had gone to a level that she never thought it would go. She knew that she loved him but she was going to have to make a choice of who she loved more. She was going to have to find a way to escape because she couldn't continue to live in fear of living in the house with her husband who was also her abuser and now her rapist. Teresa knew it was time for her to get out of the situation. She was going to have to be very smart about the situation because she knew that she wouldn't be able to take much more of his abuse.

She was starting to feel sick, so she ran to the bathroom and threw up in the toilet. She didn't know if it was the food she ate or the stress that she was under from all the abuse of her husband, but she was very sick. The house was quiet, so she assumed her husband went to work normally and left her to deal with her hurt and pain alone.

Teresa knew that she had to make a plan. She knew that it was going to be difficult because her husband made all the money and everything was in a joint bank account. She knew that her mother and she had joint accounts together just in case something went wrong, and she needed some emergency money. Well, this was it. Her face looked bad, but she knew that she was going to have to make a move while her husband was at work. She went to the room and packed as many of her clothes as she could and grabbed the keys to her car and left the house.

She didn't want to go to her mother's house because she didn't want to get her upset or get her father involved because he would try to kill her husband. She thought about going to the police station, but she didn't want to ruin her husband's image or make him lose his job. After riding around for about 30 minutes she ended up at her sister's house on the other side of town. She hadn't seen her sister since the wedding and didn't know how her sister would react. She had a key to her sister's house, but she wanted to at least warn her sister since she hadn't been around in such a long time.

She got out of the car and rang the doorbell and heard someone coming towards the door. Her sister looked out the peephole and opened the door. Her sister immediately saw her face and she hugged her and pulled her inside the house. Teresa couldn't hold back the tears as she cried tears of sorrow and pain with her sister. She was glad that her sister wasn't upset with her and the love came back as if they had never been a part.

After she stopped crying her sister said that she would get them some tea so they could catch up. She felt at home and safe with her sister. Her sister was a police officer who didn't take any junk from anyone. She knew her job and nobody bothered her because she would deal with you. She was military trained and after coming home from doing four years in the Army she joined the police department and was already a captain on the force. She was protective by nature, and she never judged anyone's situation. Teresa knew that she would be good to stay with and for her to get information on what her next move should be in her marriage.

Teresa and her sister talked for a while and her sister was caught up on when the abuse started and the incidents that led up to where they were right now. Her sister suggested that she file a restraining order against Charles and that she needed to protect herself and not go back to the house for more abuse from her husband. Her sister told her that she could stay as long as she wanted and that she was glad that she had come to her.

Teresa decided that she would tell her husband that she would not be coming back home and that she needed some time to think about where their marriage stood. Charles was very upset and said that she had better be at the house when he got home. Teresa told him that it was best that they stayed apart and that she was warning him because she was going to get a restraining order to protect herself.

She hung up on Charles because he was yelling and cursing and Teresa didn't want to hear it. She knew that she was very stressed out and she felt sick on the stomach again. She went to the bathroom and threw up again. Her sister came in to support her and asked her if she had a virus. Teresa blamed it on the stress but then thought that with everything going on she didn't remember even having a menstrual cycle this month. She thought that she may be pregnant, and she wasn't ready to be a mother, especially with a husband who was not ready to raise a child. She started crying uncontrollably and before long she felt like everything was closing in around her. She felt that she couldn't breathe and before long everything got dark, and she had fainted.

When she woke up, she was in a hospital. Her sister and her mother were in the room waiting on her to wake up and they had her under a monitor controlling her vitals. The hospital had started an IV with fluids because she was dehydrated.

Her mother was looking at her face and Teresa could tell that she had been crying and praying. Her mother had a close relationship with God and could pray to the father above. Teresa didn't know how to start, and her mother could sense it.

She said, "Baby it's going to be okay. Your family is here with you now."

Teresa felt a feeling of relief and shock because she

didn't know whether her sister or mother told her father about what was going on.

The doctor came back into the room to talk with her and made sure that it was safe to talk in front of the visitors. Teresa let them know that her mother and sister were both on her medical forms and that it was ok.

The doctor told them that she was dehydrated and that her iron and hemoglobin were low which is why she passed out. They let her know that she would probably need an iron transfusion and that she was also four weeks pregnant. The doctor said that the baby was fine but that she needed to take it easy for the next two months because it was very easy to miscarry the baby in the first trimester months.

Teresa was having mixed emotions. She should have been happy that she was pregnant by her husband, but she didn't want to be pregnant by the man who not only beat her but raped her as well. She didn't know how to handle the situation because she knew that an abortion was out of the picture. Her mother and sister were happy to learn that she was pregnant but realized that Teresa was not happy with the news. She felt that this was forced on her because she wanted to pursue her school and get a career.

The doctor told her that she would have to stay in the hospital for a little while until more tests were run, but in the meantime, they would send in a social worker to talk with her. She was nervous because she knew that she was going to have to explain the bruises on her face. She knew at this point the cat was already out of the bag and that she must tell the truth because lying was wrong by God.

Her mother and sister told her that everything would be okay and that they were glad that the situation wasn't worse. Her father did know, and he was on his way over to the hospital to see his baby girl.

Teresa felt that she had let her family down. Her mother said a prayer and told them that the social worker was ready to talk with her. Her mother and sister went out to get snacks and to wait on her daddy while she had a private talk with the social worker. She cried and told the social worker what happened and that she fled while he was at work.

The social worker told her that her sister could help her do the restraining order and that there should be no contact with her husband until he gets some help. She let her know that the restraining order was good for a year and that would give them plenty of time to see how they were going to proceed with their marriage.

Teresa knew that it was time and that when she prayed for an out, she didn't know how God would do it, but this made it possible for her to at least be around her family. She decided to do what was best to protect her and the baby and decided that she would stay with her family until she got on her own feet.

The social worker left, and she noticed that Charles had called her over eight times already in one hour. She was getting tired of this.

Teresa was in deep thought when she heard her daddy's voice. Teresa immediately started crying. Her daddy and she had a bond that nobody could explain.

He always protected her, and she knew that she should always be treated like a queen because that is how her father treated her mother and her sister.

He hugged her and all the pain went away. He told her that she didn't disappoint him and that he would always love and protect her. Her father didn't play any games when it came to any one of his girls. Her dad was never judgmental, and he always gave the answers from the Bible and not his opinion. He told her that she needed to make sure that she and the baby were safe and that she must make the best decision for herself right now. He knew that she loved her husband and wanted to make it work but that nobody could make that choice for her because they were in a marriage and everyone else needed to stay out of it. He told her to pray about it and follow and trust the Lord.

Teresa said that she would take that advice and that she wanted to get some alone time with God and maybe some more rest. Her dad kissed her and told her he loved her and that he would have her sister stay with her tonight and that he and her mother would go home to pray for her and her situation.

Teresa asked for a ginger ale and something light to put on her stomach because she noticed that she hadn't eaten anything in a while and that couldn't be good for herself or the baby. She closed her eyes and prayed to God that he would show her the next move, so she prayed and cried out and worshiped him for who he was.

Then she stayed quiet to listen, and God told her, "Now."

She was happy that she got the answer because he didn't give her one when the abuse first happened and she now knew that it was time to react. She went to sleep and got some very good rest.

She woke up and noticed that her sister was sleeping on the couch next to the window.

Teresa heard her phone buzzing on the dresser. It was Charles. She picked it up and he sounded as if he hadn't slept all night. She told him that she passed out and had been in the hospital since yesterday and that she had decided it would be best that she stay with her family a while until she figured out her next moves.

Charles started doing his regular begging, saying that it wouldn't happen again and he loved her and needed her and that he couldn't live his life without her.

Teresa listened. A part of her wanted to believe him but the other part knew that it was not true. She told him that he should get closer to God so that he could be delivered from that violent demon. Charles agreed and said that he would get some help.

She told him that the doctor also said that she was four weeks pregnant and that she needed to take it easy so that she wouldn't have a miscarriage. Charles started begging that she should come home and that she was robbing him of his bonding time with his child.

Teresa told him that this is why he really needed to get himself together because he was going to be a daddy. Teresa told him that she was getting a restraining order against him and that there would be no contact between them for one year, which would give him time to make sure that he gets himself together for their child's sake.

Charles got furious and started communicating threats over the phone. He told her that if she didn't come home with his child that it was going to be an issue and if she thought that she would keep him away from their child she had another problem coming.

Teresa's sister heard him communicating the threats and took the phone from her sister and warned him to leave her alone or there would be charges pressed against him. She told him that he was upsetting her and putting her at risk of losing the baby.

Charles calmed down because he knew Teresa's sister didn't play. That was one of the reasons why he had alienated her from her family because they were so close, and he knew they would protect their family at all costs. Charles decided that he was going to lose this fight, so he hung up the phone.

Teresa was feeling very sick. She made it to the bathroom and threw up, again. Her sister told her that she needed to eat something, and she was going to get her some breakfast. Teresa did feel a little hungry and didn't decline her sister's idea at all. Teresa knew that she would do the restraining order because her husband seemed out of control.

The doctor came back in and said that she was going to need an iron transplant and that her hemoglobin would come up if she ate more. She promised that she would eat and take better care of herself and that she would do what was best for the baby.

Her sister came back in with food and the doctor seemed happy to see it. She let her know that the nurses would be back in to get everything for the iron transplant and that they would take more blood after that so that they could check to see if everything looked good afterwards.

Teresa and her sister ate their breakfast and talked about the plan when she got out of the hospital. Her sister let her know that she would take her down to the department that will help her file a restraining order. Teresa said that she was on board to getting it done to protect herself and her child.

The nurse came back into the room with the tools she needed to do the iron transplant which would be going through her IV. She let Teresa know that this would take about two hours before all the iron would be in her, and if everything else looked good, she would be discharged today.

Her sister let her know that her mom and dad wanted everyone to stay at the house tonight to have a family night. Teresa missed how fun "family night" was with her parents. They would order pizza, watch movies and play games and talk about a lot of old memories. She was looking forward to spending time with her family. Since she had married Charles, she hadn't had any fun with her family.

She and her sister had eaten and talked until her sister and her were in the same bed together resting together. The nurse came back in to draw blood, and saw how her hemoglobin looked after eating and the iron transplant. When she drew the blood and tested it her hemoglobin was at a 7.5 which was a little better. The doctor said that she would process her discharge papers but if she had any more issues to come back to the hospital. She recommended that she follow up with her OB doctor and take iron pills and eat food with high iron.

About an hour later Teresa and her sister left the hospital heading back to her sister's house to get clothes to go spend the night at their parent's house. After they got the clothes, her sister took her to the Safe on Seven Building, which is where you file a restraining order. They got there and were able to talk with somebody right away because of her sister's badge.

Teresa told them about the incident and let them know that she just got out of the hospital today. She told them that she was not safe at home and that she had a fear of being at home with her husband. They let her know that she could meet with a judge today and see if she can get an emergency order against him and, if not, she would just have to show up in court to put it into motion. Teresa was nervous but decided that this is what she had to do. She would never have imagined being at this point in her marriage.

About an hour later she was standing in front of a judge telling her story about why she needed safety. She had the proof to show the damage because her eye was worse than it was two days ago. The judge granted an emergency order and told her not to have any contact with him and that he would be served at home or on his job so that he would be on the same page, to stay away from her.

Teresa couldn't believe that she was now a victim of domestic violence by the only man that she had ever loved. She thought about all the old times and where she was now. Her life was really upside down. When it was all over, they were heading to her parent's house to have a good time, which was more than overdue.

Her parents had already cooked the food and had gotten the cards out which included regular cards and UNO cards. The backgammon game was also out on the table which Teresa's daddy was very good at.

Teresa sat and played games with her family, and everyone was having such a good time. She sat back and her mind drifted back in time when she wasn't married to Charles and how the family and her were so close and believed in having fun and protecting one another. Her mother had prepared homemade pizza and hot wings and lots of finger foods to go with it. She put the food on the dining room table buffet style so that they could eat whatever they wanted while the games were still going on.

Teresa's dad stopped the games so that they could bless the food and everyone got food at their own pace while still playing the games. It was getting late outside, but the fun was just beginning inside.

While she was having fun with her family, Charles sat in his car thinking about when to make a move to try to get his family back. He saw his wife walk into her parents' house with her sister but decided that he had to make the right decision because her sister didn't play, and he knew she was a cop! He loved his wife and didn't want to miss another minute without her and his unborn baby. He knew that he could win his wife back; he just needed a little more time to plan. For now, he decided to go back to the house and think about what his next move should be.

It was getting late, and he figured that his wife wasn't going to come home tonight. At this point he was glad that his wife was doing ok and that he knew that she was always safe at her parents' house. He cranked his car, drove off and headed back home so that he could get some sleep for the next day.

Charles woke up and realized that he hadn't slept that well without his wife in bed with him. He could still smell her perfume on her side of the bed which caused him to miss her more. He thought that he would call her to see when she was coming home. He grabbed his phone and dialed her number only to get her voicemail. Charles tried again and got the voicemail again and got really upset. He hauled the pillow across the room and let out a loud shout. He was losing his cool, but he didn't want to lose his wife.

He decided to go shower to blow off some steam and decided that he would not go into work just in case his wife came back home today. The shower helped him to relax a little but reminded him of the memories before he had put his hands on her and the intimate moments they would have in the shower. He knew that he had to get his wife back and now that she was pregnant with their child he had to do it fast.

Charles got out of the shower, put on some workout clothing and grabbed his keys to go back to see if he could talk with his wife at her parent's house. Charles drove to the house and waited outside for a while to watch the house to see who was at her parents' house.

He noticed that her sister's car wasn't there anymore, which was a plus but noticed that her father's car was. Her father was not a pushover either and he had a set of military skills which made him dangerous which made you ensure that you were on his good side and not his bad side. He also knew that he was on the bad side, so he had to play it safe. She mentioned something about a restraining order but didn't know if it was in effect or not already.

Charles called his wife again and surprisingly she picked up the phone. Charles told her that he missed her and wanted her to come home but Teresa told him that she was coming to get some more of her things, but she was not coming to stay with him until he got some help.

Charles begged and pleaded that he would never hit her especially now that she was pregnant and that he was a changed man and only wanted to be able to protect his family. He said that he loved her and never wanted to hurt her and that he would be the best husband and father and everything she needed him to be. He begged her to just at least give him an opportunity to talk to her in person and if she wanted to she could come back and stay with her parents.

Teresa did love her husband, but she knew that he was not stable. She wanted to honor her vows and raise her family together so she thought maybe she should give him one more chance to make it right.

Teresa went into the living room to tell her father

what her decision was, and he wasn't happy at all. He begged her to pray about it some more and that he only wanted her and the baby to be safe.

Teresa said that she loved her husband and wanted to at least hear him out and see if they could work it out now that they would be having a child together. Her father told her that he couldn't make the decisions for her because she was married but he prayed that God would speak to her and that she would listen to what he was telling her to do. He told her not to let her feelings override what the Lord had said.

Teresa promised her father that she would come back if things weren't better and that she would call her mother and sister and tell them that she was going to give her marriage another chance. She called Charles and told him that he could pick her up and take her home.

Charles thanked her for giving him another chance and that he would be there in less than fifteen minutes. Charles had to make it look like he wasn't already in the neighborhood, so he drove down to the store, waited a little while then went to pick his wife up from her parent's house.

Charles walked up to the door and rang the doorbell. He waited awhile and then Teresa's daddy came to the door with a mean look on his face. Charles knew that her daddy was upset with him, so he offered an apology which he didn't accept. Her daddy was very quiet with him, and he told him that he was not welcome at his house after today. Teresa came behind her father, kissed her father and left with her husband.

Charles apologized all the way home and asked his wife how the baby was doing. Teresa didn't have much to say but she had been sick ever since she got the news. Charles got a little angry as if she was upset because she didn't want his child. He held his anger in because he didn't want anything to come in his way of getting his family back full-time, so that it could go back to the way he wanted it to go.

About twenty minutes later they were pulling back up to their house. Charles came around and opened the car door for his wife while helping her out of the car and into the house. He opened the door, and Teresa was almost scared to go in. She hadn't thought about how hard it was walking back to the place where she had been beat and raped. She let out a loud sigh and realized that God would have to help her get through this as well. Charles realized what was going on and he rubbed her shoulders and asked if she wanted to get some rest.

Teresa walked into the bedroom and her nerves caused her to get sick on the stomach. She ran in the bathroom so that she could get to the commode to throw up. She didn't know if it was her nerves or if the baby was getting the best of her. She would bet that the sickness was coming from the environment where she was raped by her husband.

Charles was very helpful with getting something cold for her forehead and helping her to sit back down. He asked her when her next appointment was and that he was very excited about being able to go. He told her that he loved her more than anything and was going to be the happiest man alive when the baby comes. Teresa was not excited about bringing a baby into the world because she knew that it was going to take up more of her time, which was going to make her put her dreams on the back burner.

Teresa told him that she had a restraining order that she needed to drop if they were going to try one last time. Charles said that it needed to be dropped that day so that they wouldn't get in any trouble being together. Teresa agreed and said that they could go right now because she loved him and wanted their relationship to work, especially since the baby was coming.

Teresa and Charles went to the magistrate's office to drop the restraining order. The magistrate looked at Teresa's face and asked Charles to wait outside. When they got a part, the magistrate asked her if she was doing this on her own free will or was she in any danger right now. Teresa told her that she was doing this on her own and that she loved her husband and wanted it to work. The magistrate told her that if she dropped the restraining order she would not be able to take out another one. Teresa told them that she understood and wanted to drop it anyway. Teresa didn't listen to what God had said because she allowed her feelings to look over reality.

The magistrate fulfilled her request and Teresa left to find her husband. They went back home, and Charles seemed to be in a good mood after she dropped the order. He told her that she had made the right decision by fighting for their family.

Charles and Teresa pulled back up at home and they

decided that they would cook dinner inside and spend some quality time with each other. They talked about everything and ate dinner together. Charles and she laid on the bed while he gave her a massage and rubbed on their baby.

Teresa was almost asleep when she felt that Charles had more sexual plans. Teresa felt that it was too soon after all that had happened in the last couple of weeks, so she told Charles not right now. Charles got upset and told her that she was his wife and that she needed to fulfill his desires! He had been without it for weeks and that she should be glad that he didn't cheat on her!

Teresa knew that she couldn't get in that mood to do that after what she had just gone through with him. She told Charles that she wasn't feeling that well and if he could give her one more day to rest.

Charles got madder and pushed her down on her back and got on top of her so he could get what he wanted. Teresa tried to fight but Charles put his hand around her neck holding her too tightly. Teresa couldn't breathe but Charles was too caught up on getting what he wanted. She fought a little more, then her body went limp.

Charles was already inside of her getting what he wanted when he realized his wife was motionless and not saying or moaning at all. When he got off of her, he realized that it was blood all in the bed and his wife was not breathing. He shook her, calling her name but there was still no answer!

Charles started to panic and didn't know if he should call the police or not. He called the police and told them that his wife was not moving and that he thought that she was having a miscarriage. Charles held Teresa's body in his arms praying that she would be okay. Charles didn't want to, but he called her father and told him, and her father relayed the message to the rest of her family. Her daddy got off the phone and called the police and told the police to meet him at his daughter's address.

It felt like forever, but Charles then heard sirens coming down the street. He went into the living room and opened the door and went back in to support his wife. When the paramedics got there, they immediately started CPR while asking questions. Charles answered the questions leaving out the part where he raped his wife and strangled her to death.

Another 20 minutes went by, and Teresa had not come back yet, and her family was running in the door yelling and trying to get to Charles. They knew that he had finally taken their loved one from them. Her father and mother were screaming and praying and then two police cars came on the scene. Her sister got out of one and ran into the house while the other cop came in to see what was going on.

Her sister was crying but trying to do her job efficiently. She told her parents that Teresa was gone to be with the Lord and the house was now a crime scene which meant no one could leave until the investigation was over. The other cop put handcuffs on Charles and put him in the back of the police car. They pronounced her dead and put the time on paper. Before long the house was yellow taped, and the forensic team and more detectives were on the scene in no time. They made Teresa's sister stay with her family because she was too close to the investigation.

The detectives did their jobs by separating everyone and asking questions about what may have led to this. Everyone had their stories but the father told them that she had just left today and said that she was going to give him another chance, but she had just gotten out of the hospital from him beating her and she found out that she was pregnant. They told the detectives that he was very violent and that they wanted an autopsy because he was not telling the truth about what happened to their loved one.

After all their stories were taken the detectives told them that they had to finish getting any evidence from the room and that they could go outside and wait until they were done in there.

Her family couldn't believe that their baby girl had been taken by the hands of her own husband. She only wanted to be a good wife which only gave her a short life.

Her mother called Charles' mother and told her what had happened, and Charles' mother was very sad for everyone. She knew that her son had anger issues like his father, and she knew what Teresa may have been going through marrying her son. She told Charles' father who was all worried about where his son was like he was supposed to be anywhere but at the police station.

The news crew had heard, and they were there trying to get the story as well. Several hours passed and the father told them where they wanted the body to be moved and what hospital.

Their family was not handling grief well at all, but they knew that God would get them through it all.

Neighbors were all out looking and hoping everyone was ok but after seeing the black bag with a body in it, they thought the worse. Detectives were asking neighbors questions about their relationship which some neighbors told them that this wasn't the first time they were having some domestic problems. They finally finished up at the house, took the body to the hospital for an autopsy and left the family grieving over their loved one.

Charles was at the police station in a room, demanding that he get a drink of water and a phone call. He was pacing back and forth trying to think of a way to get out of it. He remembered when he was in college, and he had put his hand on his ex-girlfriend. His father told him not to say anything without his lawyer present.

Charles didn't mean to do it. He just wanted to be intimate with his wife. How could this happen like this? He was just about to be a father and now he wasn't even a husband anymore. Charles started crying realizing all this time his wife told him to get some professional help, and he didn't stay in it. He realized that he was really a monster and had turned into the man who treated his mother the same way which was also his father.

He cried and cried and told the officer that he wanted to confess. He knew that with his behavior he didn't need another child like him and he needed to be put away so he couldn't hurt anyone else. The detective came in and told him to tell him everything that happened. Charles told him about the first incident that caused his wife to go stay with her parents and to get the restraining order on him. He told the officer that he loved his wife and never wanted to hurt her, especially when she told him that she was pregnant. Charles told the detective that he had tried to force his wife to make love to him, but he didn't know his own strength. He told the detective that his hand was around her neck while he was trying to make love to her and that is when he saw that the bed was covered with blood and that she was not moving. He mentioned that he called the police, but he was scared of what was going to happen to him. He confessed to everything and told them that he never meant for it to happen like this and that he missed and loved his wife.

The detective had his recorded confession and told him to stand and put his hands behind his back. The cop put him in cuffs and took him to a jail cell. In the meantime, his father and lawyer came to help and noticed that it was too late, and his son had already confessed to killing his wife. Charles didn't want to see his father and felt that it was his fault that he was like that in the first place. Charles was charged with one count of first-degree murder.

One Month Later....

The coroner called and told her family that the autopsy had come back, and they all went to find out what they already knew. The detective told the family that Charles confessed to everything and was charged with two counts of first-degree murder. The autopsy confirmed that she died by strangulation and the baby was about three months old. The coroner also told them that she had trauma in her vagina confirming that he raped her brutally and she died from not getting enough oxygen to her brain.

The family was torn even more to know that their good little girl was only trying to be the best wife and mother that she could be. The coroner let them know that the body would be at the funeral home by tomorrow and they could now start to bury their loved one properly. This was a very sad occasion because their daughter didn't even get to live a long life.

Charles was charged and sentenced to life in prison. His mother was very sad that the two families were ruined by domestic violence. This caused Charles's father to start abusing his wife more often which she decided that it was now time for her to leave so she wouldn't end up like her son's deceased wife. She had been trying to remain a good wife for her son's sake but it only got her still taking abuse and her son in jail for killing his wife because of all he had seen them go through when he was younger.

She got a restraining order against her husband, took enough money to make it and moved out of town to be back with her own family. She loved her son but knew that she had to save herself first. She planned to come see him after she ensured her own safety.

Charles's mother was so sad for Teresa's family that she sent them a large check in the mail to cover all the expenses for the funeral and for their pain and suffering. She didn't attend the funeral but heard that it was a blessed homegoing service. She knew that Teresa had always been a good girl and knew that she was too good for her own son. She had only wished that her son would have gone through counseling and got himself right but now it was too late. She loved her son but knew that her son needed counseling to be free from his father's demons. She blamed herself for not leaving earlier and deciding to stay with her husband so that she and her son would be supported. She now regretted every day that she stayed, because she had years of abuse and it still didn't change.

One Year Later….

Teresa's family was getting over things day by day and knew that they would always cherish her. One thing that they never had to question was where Teresa's soul would spend eternity. She was very close to God and always strived to live like the Bible said you were supposed to live.

Teresa's family decided to open up a domestic violence women's support group where women could get safe help, talk with counselors and even get help with relocating to a safe place. Her father knew that Teresa would have wanted to help others and Charles' mother had gotten help and was also an advocate to help women in domestic violence relationships. She wanted to help young women understand that taking care of yourself had to be first.

Teresa's sister talked with women and shared her

story on how she lost her sister to domestic violence by the hands of her own husband and how important it was to utilize the law and not take advantage of the restraining orders. She showed reports of how so many women start the restraining order but then drop them only to be abused again and again, or even killed by the hand of their lovers.

Teresa's father went to see Charles in prison to forgive him and even had started mentoring him and helping him get his relationship back with God. Teresa's family knew that God was bigger than any situation and that you have to forgive anyone that do you wrong so that God can forgive you in heaven. Every day each one of Teresa's family was healing every day and Charles' mother was also healing and counseling showed her how to heal and value her own self-worth. She learned what real love was and what it wasn't and realized that she wasn't loved by her husband, only controlled.

Despite how the situation ended up, Teresa's legacy was left behind helping others to learn to recognize the signs of abuse and how to deal with it earlier than later. Teresa's family knew that even though their family member had been called home to live with the Lord too early for them, it was important to be able to forgive the ones that wronged them so that they could one day see her again.

THE END

If you are in an abusive relationship or marriage, please do what is best to protect yourself and your children, if you have any. There are numbers you can call that can help you. Reach out to someone that you can trust! A start would be:
—National Domestic Violence Hotline, 1 800 799-7233, or text to BEGIN to 88788

ACKNOWLEDGEMENTS

I first want to give all honor to my Lord above who is the beginning and end of my life. He is the one who made it all possible to get this far and to make me aware of who I am in him. I want to honor my husband who always stood behind me no matter what I decided to do. It was him who inspired me to write a book and now I am writing another. I want to thank my Pastor and first Lady and my New Life Community Church family for always supporting me and holding me accountable for being who I am in Christ.

I thank my sons for allowing me to be able to lead them back to Christ. I want to then thank my mom for being a strong mother who put great qualities in me. She pushed me to be better than the rest and gave me big responsibilities at a young age because she believed in me. I want to thank my sisters and my two best friends for being on my team and the close bond that we will always have. Each one of them did their part by pushing me and letting me know that they were proud of what I was doing.

I want to thank the members of Empower Publishing for getting me out there and having patience with me while I embrace becoming an author. Last but not certainly least, I would like to thank each one of my fans, women and men for believing in me and purchasing my book because you are who I am writing for. I love each one of you and can't wait to hear your thoughts on the book.

ABOUT THE AUTHOR

My name is Tamelia Keaton known as Mia. I was born in Winston-Salem, NC. My mother is a strong woman who is also a nurse. My mom had 4 girls, however my daddy has 7 children. I have a total of 5 sisters and 1 brother, and I have been residing in Winston-Salem all my life. Even though I was raised up without my biological father my mother ensured that she put the right qualities in my sisters and I so that we could be successful.

I am married to Miguel Keaton who is a disabled Veteran and one of the best Godsent men there is. I have two biological sons but together we have 5 sons and 1 bonus son. I have a large family which includes a lot of strong women who were empowering to me as a person.

I am a person who loves traveling to see different places with my family, Zumba with my Zumba family, hanging out with my church family and writing in my spare time.

I went to Carver High School where I obtained my diploma and enjoyed running track. I obtained my Bachelor's degree graduating Cum Laude in Healthcare Management with a specialization in Gerontology from American Intercontinental University in Atlanta Georgia and pledging to be a part of Alpha Sigma Lambda, the Honors Society club as well.

Tamelia Keaton

I have had a long career with Food Lion having the pleasure to be a Customer Service Manager and managing a frontend. I have also had the honors of working for Wells Fargo Bank where I experienced every role in retail banking and having the pleasure to become a Branch Manager at one of the locations in Winston-Salem. I now enjoy writing, reading and supporting my own family.

I enjoy motivating others to bring out their boldness and discovering their purpose for the body of Christ. I am a person who loves to serve wherever my skills are needed and now I am an author who likes to write books about things that may have happened in my life to help others who may be going through it. Look out for more books in the future. I am on a mission and that mission is to help as many people as possible get it right before the Lord comes back.

www.ingramcontent.com/pod-product-compliance
Lightning Source LLC
Chambersburg PA
CBHW070748180626
46818CB00007B/3038